Ben Davis is the author of many funny books for children and teenagers, including *My Dad Is Definitely Not a Crime Lord*, *The Private Blog of Joe Cowley*, and the multi-award-winning *The Soup Movement.* Before becoming a published author, Ben wrote jokes and sketches for radio shows. These days, Ben lives with his wife and two children in Staffordshire, and when he's not writing or visiting schools he also works as a postman.

bendavis_86
@bendavis_86
bendavisauthor

Published in the UK by Scholastic, 2023
1 London Bridge, London, SE1 9BG
Scholastic Ireland, 89E Lagan Road,
Dublin Industrial Estate, Glasnevin, Dublin, D11 HP5F

ISBN 978 0702 31578 7

A CIP catalogue record for this book
is available from the British Library.

Printed and bound in Great Britain by Clays Ltd, Elcograf S.p.A
Paper made from wood grown in sustainable forests
and other controlled sources.

1 3 5 7 9 10 8 6 4 2

www.scholastic.co.uk

My BRILLIANT PLAN to FIX EVERYTHING

BEN DAVIS

SCHOLASTIC

For all the posties.

Chapter One

"Lighten up, will you?" says Mum, jabbing at me with the greasy barbecue tongs. "This is a Norris family tradition!"

I mean, she's right. We always have a barbecue on the first day of the summer holidays. But every year up until now it's been me, my older sister Indie, Mum and Dad. This is the first year with no Dad and, as far as I'm concerned, with no Dad, there's no barbecue.

He loved being in charge of that thing. He'd flip burgers high into the air and catch them on his spatula; he'd sing super loudly and out of tune, using a ladle as a microphone; he'd wear his embarrassing buff-dude apron and wink at Mum. It was fun. Not only that, it was the Natural Order of Things: comfortable and familiar. Since he left, everything has gone out of whack, and I feel like I'm on a disintegrating spaceship, falling deeper and deeper into the void.

"Remind me why Dad couldn't be here again," I say, putting down my half-eaten burger, which doesn't taste anywhere near as good as usual.

"You know why," Mum sing-songs, a forced cheerfulness stuck to her voice like sauce on ribs. "Now who wants a hot dog?"

"Just the sausage for me," says Indie, holding up her plate without looking up from her phone. "I'm doing keto."

I don't know what keto is, nor do I care. Maybe it means being an absolute nightmare? Because she has been worse than ever in the month since Dad left. She only wears black now. She says it's because she's "in mourning for our family unit". Seriously? I mean, I am too, but I don't need to change my clothes for it. She reckons that, at seventeen, she's had five more years than me with Dad so she misses him more, but I reckon it's just because she *loves* attention.

"Look at that," Mum says, nodding at the setting sun in the distance. Our street is at the top of a big hill, so we get a nice view of the woods far away and the canal glimmering in the sunlight. Dad used to sit outside with a drink and say he was "surveying his kingdom". That was before he changed a year or so ago and the Natural Order of Things began to fall apart.

"You know what they say about red sky at night, don't you?" Mum asks, dead boringly.

I think she expects me or Indie to say something, but we keep quiet. This is more like a wake than a barbecue.

Mum blows at a stray strand of hair in front of her eyes, but it just flops back to where it was. "Shepherd's delight!" Mum is an estate agent, so it's her job to make dumps seem like palaces. She can't manage it with this situation though. "And you know what they say about red sky in the morning, don't you?" she goes on.

"Nuclear apocalypse?" says Indie, which makes me laugh. Wow, she can be funny when she wants to be.

"Indie!" Mum scolds her. "And, Alex, don't encourage her."

Great, she makes the crack and I still end up getting told off. What a life. I check my right pocket. Phone: *present*. I check my left pocket. Wallet: *present*. I don't know why I even own a wallet. It's not like I really have money. All that's in there is a card that gets me into the local leisure centre and a couple of train tickets from a year ago. But still, they have to be present. It is the Natural Order of Things.

"Hello?"

A voice comes from the other side of the gate and I recognize it straight away.

"Dad!" I jump to my feet as Dad reaches over, pulls down the bolt and walks into the garden. He's wearing a suit I last saw him wear for my cousin's wedding about five years ago, and it looks like it's about to burst. He's also brushed his hair and had a shave, but he must have caught himself with the razor because he has a tiny piece of tissue stuck to his chin, blobbed red in the middle. In his hand, he swings a plastic bag.

"I can't believe you're doing the Norris family summer barbecue without me!" he says in this really overly jolly way.

"Carl," says Mum, her own fake happiness long gone, "we talked about this."

But Dad ignores her and marches over to the

grill. "What's this?" he says, poking at the empty burger box. "Own brand? Well, that simply won't do."

He reaches into the bag and pulls out a load of meat, slapping it down on the little barbecue table. "This is from Wilson's Butchers in Fishwick. I've known the old man for years so he gives me the top stuff. Only the best for this family."

"Carl," Mum warns again.

Dad bends over to me and Indie, giving us both kisses on our foreheads. This *should* be the Natural Order of Things, but it's off. It's like I'm looking at it through a funhouse mirror.

"Look, I know I was miserable, Kate, I do," says Dad. "But I've changed. Look at me!"

Mum does look at him as he stands there, his arms stretched wide. "You think putting on an old suit and buying some meat is just going to fix everything?" she says.

Dad's arms slap back down to his sides. He looks deflated. "Of course I don't, but it's a start, isn't it?"

Mum puts down her tongs and rubs her forehead, leaving a charcoal stain. "We've been through this so many times, Carl; I don't know when it's going to sink in."

"I know," says Dad, "but hear me out."

"I'm not sure I want to," says Mum, leaning down to us. "Kids, can you go inside, please? I don't want you hearing all of this."

"No way!" I say. "I want Dad here."

"Me too," says Indie. "Besides, there's no way I can get any more traumatized than I already am."

Even though we're on the same side in this moment, she's still the most annoying person on Earth.

"I said, can you *please* go inside." Mum raises her voice now.

"They're my children too, Kate!" Dad pipes up.

And then they proceed to have their argument: the same one I heard play out time and time again over the year before they separated. The one where Dad would go on about how desperately unhappy he was and Mum, to begin with, would try and help, but then would run out of ways and just get fed up, and that made Dad say nasty things, and then Mum would say nasty things back, and no amount of me tidying my room and making sure all my things were in their exact spot would stop it.

"Look, Carl, I know you're disappointed with how your life has turned out. I know you didn't want to be a postman for twenty years, and I know you had these grand dreams about being a writer," Mum says. "But you know what writers do? They write. They don't sit around complaining."

"Listen, I'm busy," Dad says. "And by the time I finish work, I'm too tired."

Mum laughs, but there's no warmth and she's barely even smiling. "Well, then I don't know what to tell you, Carl. I don't know what to tell you."

Chapter Two

I wanted to go and stay at Dad's last night, but Mum put her foot down, and, anyway, Dad is staying in the granny flat at Uncle Pete's house. I'd have to sleep either on the floor or in Dad's bed with him, and I wasn't really keen on either. Since Mum and Dad started having problems, I gave myself a set bedtime every night. At that exact time I watch one episode of a selection of six approved shows before turning off the TV and going to sleep. If I slept over at Dad's, that would all get disrupted.

So that's why I'm on my bike now, at seven thirty in the morning, on my way to see him at work. I know I can wait until after he finishes, but this is too urgent.

Dad works in a little village outside town called

Fishwick. There's nothing exciting there: just a load of houses, some shops, a park and tons of pubs. Plus, it's built on two huge hills, which means that, no matter where you walk, you'll end up gasping for breath by the time you get there. Bad planning, if you ask me.

The quickest way to Fishwick from our house in Tammerstone is to head down our street and then bike along the canal: straight line all the way, and if you can avoid people fishing and gangs of old ladies jogging at a glacial pace, you'll make it in good time. My personal best is fifteen minutes, thirty-seven seconds.

Luckily, this morning the towpath is clear and the air is warm and soft like a blanket. Perfect weather. Normally during holidays I'd be doing something with my best friend, Spencer, but he is spending the entire summer at his grandparents' house in France. I was supposed to be going for a couple of weeks, but with everything that's happened I couldn't get my parents to agree on it, and now it's too late. An entire summer on my own, it is, then. Again, very much not the Natural Order of Things. My spaceship has lost communication with ground control.

But this morning, I have decided that things are going to change. I no longer care that Spencer is away the whole time, because even if he was here, I wouldn't have time to hang out with him. No, this summer is about one thing and one thing only: I have to get Mum and Dad back together. Someone has to restore the Natural Order of Things, and as no one else seems willing or able, it's going to have to be down to me.

Surely it can't be that hard. They loved each other before, didn't they? They must have! They went through all the trouble of getting married, then having Indie, realizing they'd made a terrible mistake and having me to make up for it. All they have to do is remember what they loved about each other.

Thing is, it's all Dad. He's totally the reason they split. He had been fine, his usual happy self, but then he went to some ridiculous school reunion. He saw an old friend who was basically a millionaire and that made Dad feel like the world's biggest loser.

After that, he became miserable. We all tried to cheer him up, even Indie. We let him turn on his radio station in the car for once; we watched his favourite films with him; I even pretended to be into football. Nothing worked. Instead, he got angry at himself, then he got angry at us and, well, I guess Mum just had enough.

So the way I see it is: it's my job to get Dad back to the person he once was. And the answer to *that* is in my bag right now, thudding against my back. Once he has this, he'll bounce back and then all he'll have to do is show Mum that it's for real and not just, as she put it last night, "trying to stick a plaster over a severed limb", and we'll be back to normal. Maybe even Indie will stop being such a nightmare with her funeral clothes and her tippety-tap-tapping away at miserable poetry on a typewriter she bought from a charity shop.

I allow myself to drift off and daydream about what it will be like. Dad will be back in the kitchen, cooking dinner for when Mum gets home from work. He'll have his music blasting and I won't even complain that it's ancient and terrible. I won't take any of it for granted ever again. I won't—

WHOA!

A flash of black darts in front of my bike. I pump the brakes out of instinct, then I immediately see what's going to happen. I'm going to flip over the handlebars and land in the canal: the disgusting, brown, murky canal. My back wheel lifts off the ground and I'm going, I'm going…

CLANK!

OK, maybe I'm not. The wheel slams back to the ground, sending a jolt through my entire body. Well, that could have been worse. I look down at the cause of my near miss and see a black cat staring up at me as if it's all my fault.

"Watch where you're going," I say to the cat, as if it can understand me.

The cat glares back like it wants to follow me home and murder me, and I start to feel uneasy.

"Pssssst. Madge," a whisper comes from somewhere. "Get back in here."

It's only now I properly notice the barge moored up just a few paces away. It looks like it's seen better days, with a flaking painted sign that says *Lola*, surrounded by sun-bleached roses.

Whoever heard of a cat living on a boat, anyway? Don't they hate water? This cat eventually slinks out of my way and squeezes back on to the boat through an open shutter. I lean down and see a girl staring out. Her mouth is a moody straight line and her face is pale like a vampire's, surrounded by bright red hair.

"Your cat nearly lost one of its nine lives just then," I say.

The girl says nothing and slams the shutter closed. Wow, really friendly. See, this is what happens when I try and make jokes. Never mind. No time to make friends. Sorting Dad is all that matters.

Shaking my head and thanking my lucky stars I didn't end up in the disgusting sludge trench they call a canal, I push off from the path and climb the slope to the Fishwick Bridge that leads to the village.

The primary school is eerily quiet, a big banner that says "SEE YOU IN SEPTEMBER" flapping gently in the breeze. Dad's depot is down a track just on the other side. Well, calling it a depot makes it sound grander than it actually is. It's more of a shack, about the size of a garage. The main depot is in Tammerstone's town centre, and they have to bring Fishwick's mail and parcels down to the shack every morning. Dad prefers working in Fishwick. He says it means his boss isn't breathing down his neck all the time; his boss only comes down to Fishwick once a month, if that. Dad's never been keen on bosses, but his new one especially winds him up. I think he's part of the reason Dad's so miserable.

I find the door to the depot already open when I get there. Either because it's a warm day, or someone has farted. Maybe both, actually. I can hear a radio advert for a car showroom burbling away. It's the same advert I hear every time I go there. One of the official rules of the Fishwick depot is that no one touches the radio. It has been tuned to Classic Indie Rock 105 since dinosaurs roamed the Earth.

"Here he is!" Dad roars as he sees me, pulling me in for a headlock. See, that's the thing with Dad when he's at work: you'd never know anything is wrong.

The depot consists of only two rooms: a toilet, which always has a spider the size of my face in it, and the main sorting area, which has three fittings similar to big shelving units, each one allocated to a round. Each fitting has a slot for every address on the round. Dad and the other two staff members – Miriam and Lloyd, both quite a bit older – have to put letters in their corresponding slots and the parcels on shelves above. Then, when it's all done, they bundle the letters together with elastic bands and bag everything up. They're still sorting them now.

"The prodigal son," says Lloyd in his typical friendly growl. He says that every time he sees me, but I'm not sure I know what it means. I'm not certain he does, either. Even though he's probably nearly my granddad's age, there's something cool about Lloyd. It might be because he always wears a bandana, or has old Navy tattoos, or the fact that the top of his left index finger up to the second knuckle is missing and he comes up with a different story for how he lost it every time I see him.

When Dad finally lets me go, he has a huge smile on his face. You'd have no idea he trudged out of our garden with tears in his eyes last night.

"So what are you doing here, son?" he says.

Miriam chuckles as she tosses a small box on to a shelf. "If he's anything like my boys, he's here to ask you for money."

Dad laughs and pulls out his pockets so they dangle by his sides. "Good luck with that, my lad."

I laugh along and check my own pockets. Phone.

Present. Wallet. *Present*. "No, it's nothing like that," I say.

"I know why he's here," says Lloyd. "He's come to show us his special talent!"

Dad and Miriam cheer. "Yeah, that's it," says Dad. "Go on, give us a blast, Alex."

I sigh. Basically, my one and only talent is that I can do a really good impression of a monkey, and they make me do it every time I'm there. I realized I could do it when I was about five, and because it always earned applause, attention and sometimes money and/or sweets, I was incentivized to get better at it. Now, I wish I'd never bothered. There's something weird about a twelve-year-old pretending to be a gibbon. Still, it doesn't look like I'm getting out of it, so I take a breath, give them a "ooh, ooh, ooh" and a big screech. It earns, as I was fully expecting, a round of applause. The Natural Order of Things.

"What do you reckon, Lloydy?" Dad yells. "What score do you give him?"

Lloyd responds by holding up both hands, fingers outstretched.

"Not bad," says Dad, nodding. "Nine and a half."

Miriam cackles at that, and Lloyd launches

himself across the tiny room and hits Dad with a soft karate chop.

"I'll have you know I lost this finger in the jaws of a great white after my ship sank in the middle of the Pacific."

Dad hits back with his own chop. "That's funny. Last week, it was an escaped tiger."

"And the week before that, a hungry seagull," says Miriam.

"You'll find out the real story one day," Lloyd says, going back to his fitting. "And when you do, it'll blow your minds!"

When Lloyd and Miriam finally go back to their work, sorting letters into slots, Dad lowers his voice to talk to me. "Everything all right?"

"Well, not really," I say.

Dad stops what he's doing and looks at me. The face he'd put on for the others is gone and now his droopy eye bags look much bigger.

"You'll be OK, son," he whispers, giving my arm a quick squeeze. "I shouldn't have come around last night. I made a fool of myself."

"No, we wanted you there," I say.

But Dad shakes his head. "No. I need to stay away. Your mum's made up her mind."

My stomach twists like a wrung-out pair of swimming trunks. How can he just accept things so easily? Where is his fight? I have to turn him around.

He glances at Lloyd and Miriam, then nods at the door. "Come on. Let's talk outside."

I follow Dad out into the little car park, where Lloyd and Miriam's shared van and Dad's trolley sit nestled together. My bike is chained up behind it. Dad leans on a corrugated iron fence and lets out a sigh that sounds like a slow puncture. "I'm surprised your mother let you come here after yesterday."

I cringe a little. Ever since they started having problems, they've been referring to each other as "your mother" and "your father". It's like living in *Downton Abbey.*

"Well, she doesn't actually know," I say. "But that doesn't matter. I was thinking about what you two were talking about and it gave me an idea."

Dad wrinkles his already wrinkled forehead. "Oh yeah?"

"Well, what Mum said about you wanting to write books," I say. "I mean, it's not like you need fancy equipment for that, right? It's not like skiing or nuclear fusion. All you need is a computer to write on."

Dad sighs again and scratches the back of his neck. "Right. And at the moment, I don't even have that."

I take off my backpack and unzip it. "I went up the loft and found this," I say, pulling out our old laptop. "It's a bit slow, but it still works. And it's got a word processor on it. As long as you save regularly, you'll be fine."

Dad smiles and his eyes go watery. I've seen Dad cry a few times these past few months and I hate it, I hate it, I hate it. The total opposite of the Natural Order of Things.

"Oh, Alex, that's so thoughtful of you," he says, then rubs his face, like something's heavy on his mind. "You know, I think this might be the machine I started writing a book on years ago."

"Really?" I say. "What was the book called?"

"*The Last Letter*," says Dad, chuckling shyly. "They say write what you know, don't they?"

"How come you didn't finish it?"

Dad turns the laptop over in his hands, like it's an antique. "Life stuff. Work, football, you kids. There just aren't enough hours in the day." He gulps and I hear his throat click. "At least with me living in Uncle Pete's granny flat, this will give me something to do rather than fall asleep in front of the TV."

I think about Dad sitting in that sad little outbuilding, still decorated as if an old lady lives there, eating his microwave dinners off his lap, and I have to turn away so he can't see my eyes watering too.

As I do, I see a car swinging into the car park. It weaves around the van and heaves to a stop right next to us.

"Ugh, it's Peregrine," Dad groans quietly without moving his lips.

Dad's boss, who he's been moaning about for the last year or so. For a start, Peregrine's younger than Dad by about twenty years. Secondly, he brought with him a load of changes Dad didn't like. Now they have hand-held scanners that track their every move and flag if they have too long a break or stop and chat with too many people. Dad once said he wanted to get rich just so he could buy a helicopter and throw his scanner into an active volcano.

"That man," Dad would say every night at

dinner, jabbing the table with his index finger, "is all about the shareholders. He couldn't give a fig about providing a public service. Profit, profit, profit, that's all he cares about."

Peregrine swishes out of his big, shiny car and nods at Dad briskly. He's very short. Like, I'm twelve and I'm the same height as him. And there's nothing wrong with being short, but this guy seems to do everything he can to make himself look bigger. His hair is brushed back into an immense bouffant, his shoes have soles as thick as bricks and the shoulders on his suit jacket are so padded he looks like one of those American football players.

"Henryyyyy," he says, the name sliding out of his mouth somehow sounding greasy.

Dad shuffles uneasily. "I go by my middle name, Peregrine," he says. "It's Carl, remember?"

Peregrine ignores this and pulls a sheet of paper out of a neat black folder in his hands. He glances down at the laptop, then at me. "I'm sorry, have I interrupted an IT support meeting?"

"This is my son, Alex," says Dad. "He was just bringing me this from home. You know how things are. We spoke about it."

"Ah yes, your divorce," says Peregrine.

"Separation," Dad corrects him.

Peregrine shrugs his enormous stuffed shoulders. "Tomayto, tomahto. Anyway, let's cut to the chase, shall we?" He stiffly flicks the piece of paper. "We've had a complaint."

Dad sighs. "Was it Greenwood?"

Ah, Mr Greenwood. I remember Dad moaning about him too. Always complaining about something, never satisfied, loves his garden more than his wife, yada yada yada.

Peregrine nods. "Bingo. So what's the score, Henry? Mr Greenwood here says you were rude to him."

Dad shakes his head. "I can explain."

"I was hoping you'd say that," says Peregrine, with a smirk. "As you know, rude behaviour or language towards our customers is a very serious matter and reflects on us badly as a brand."

I see Dad flinch. I can almost hear his brain screaming, *We're not a brand, we're a SERVICE!*

"Hence why I am here in person," Peregrine continues. "It's important you understand the gravity of the sitch."

This is the first time I have met Peregrine and I already see that Dad wasn't exaggerating at all.

“Sitch”? Why not just say “situation”? It’s not that much longer.

“Mr Greenwood says you said, and I quote, ‘don’t get sassy with me, you old goblin’.”

Dad goes pale. “But how did he? I didn’t … oh no.”

Peregrine nods smugly. “Digital doorbell.”

Dad hates those things. They record everything you do at the doorstep. He says it makes him feel like he’s being spied on. “It’s *Big Brother*!” he’d say. “You can’t even scratch your backside without someone watching!”

“Look, I didn’t think he’d hear that,” says Dad to Peregrine. “He was giving me a hard time about delivering pizza leaflets, even though, as you know, we have to deliver them.”

“I appreciate you were doing your job correctly,” says Peregrine, “but you can’t just go around saying everything that pops into your head.”

“I know,” says Dad, clutching the laptop to his chest and staring at the floor. “Sorry, Peregrine.” He looks just like me when I get told off. It’s weird.

“Sure you are, Hen-man, but we have to follow procedures,” says Peregrine, pulling out a phone so new I don’t even think it’s out yet. “So I have no choice but to set the wheels in motion for a formal meeting about giving you a warning."

Dad groans. "Don't you think that's a bit over the top?"

"What I think is immaterial, Henny," he says. "I have to stick to the letter of the law, you know that."

Just then I sense a presence behind me. "I heard all of that," Lloyd says, his voice even more gravelly than normal. "And for someone who's so into procedures, you don't seem to know them very well."

"Ah, Mr Lloyd," says Peregrine, in the same way supervillains greet captured spies. "Always a pleasure."

Lloyd grunts. "Whatever, sunshine. You know as well as I do that Carl needs union representation for anything like this and, as his union rep, I'm telling you that you need to put it all in writing so we can respond accordingly."

The word "accordingly" sounds weird coming out of Lloyd, but it's obvious he knows what he's talking about from the way Peregrine's face has gone from lottery-winning smug to just-swigged-curdled-milk sick. "I think you'll find—" he starts.

"That I'm right. Now if you'll excuse us, some

people in this company have to actually graft for a living. Come on, Carl." Lloyd rests his four-and-half-fingered hand on Dad's shoulder and guides him back inside. I follow and watch as Peregrine stares after us, then gets in his car and peels away.

"Don't worry about Greenwood," says Lloyd. "Me and him go way back. I'll make him drop it. If he doesn't, I'll tell his wife about..." Lloyd stops and looks at me like he's just remembered I'm there. "... about something or other."

They all go back to their fittings, Lloyd grumbling about how he has pants older than Peregrine, and I'm relieved that at least Dad has someone looking out for him here at work.

Carl felt energized after finishing his round that day, which was very unusual. Normally, he would flop into his car with a big "oof", then drive home and crash on the sofa for the rest of the day. Not today, though. Today would be the start of a new Carl. That disastrous barbecue last night had crushed his spirit, but his boy, his sweet Alex, had brought it back to life. Reminded him that not everyone had given up on him.

He got back to the granny flat and looked at

his surroundings. He had let this place fall into disrepair. The shelves were thick with dust and the carpets were speckled with crisp crumbs and bits of fried rice from the takeaway, as well as several substances he couldn't confidently identify. He couldn't let that continue. If he was going to turn his life around, he should begin with his home. It wasn't exactly the Ritz, but the least he could do was make it less of a rubbish dump. As soon as that was right, he could sit down and start work on his book.

After dusting, polishing, pushing the antique vacuum cleaner around and doing the washing-up and drying, Carl was still full of beans. He felt young again, ready to take on the world.

"That's it!" he said to no one. "I'm going out for a run!"

Carl squeezed on a pair of shorts and a T-shirt and headed out, starting at a good pace as he left his brother's front garden. Sure, he'd already walked sixteen kilometres that day, but what's a few more. He fired up the theme from *Rocky* on his headphones, and aimed a few punches at the air as he went.

Maybe this is the new me? he thought. *Maybe I'll*

become a runner? Maybe I'll do a marathon? Yes. That's what I'll do. I'm going to train for a marathon. The kids and Kate won't believe it!

Then he got a stitch and had to stop, and as soon as he did, his knees started to scream in pain.

OK, so maybe running's not for me, he thought as he desperately tried to suck air back into his lungs barely a full kilometre from where he started. *But that doesn't mean I can't keep fit in other ways.*

Carl headed home, walking slowly this time, and having ordered himself a takeaway as a treat.

Chapter Three

I've given Dad a couple of days to get started. I know it can take a while for your imagination to get firing.

So now I'm back on my bike heading over to Uncle Pete's. He lives the other side of Fishwick. My personal best getting there is twenty-four minutes and three seconds. I don't think I'll manage it today though, because Mum made cottage pie for dinner and it's weighing down my stomach like a bowling ball. Still I press on.

The sky is a gentle light purple and the air is still as a pond. I could take the canal to Uncle Pete's, but after I nearly got killed by that cat, I take the roadway. As I go over the canal bridge, I see that *Lola* boat is still there. The cat sits on the roof, basking in the late afternoon sun, and I catch a glimpse of the red-haired girl walking towards the boat, carrying a plastic shopping bag. Does she actually live on that thing? I don't think I've ever met someone who lives on a boat before. My grandparents sometimes go on barge holidays, but I couldn't imagine being on one permanently. Where would you keep all your stuff?

After arriving in a disappointing twenty-seven minutes and fifteen seconds, I find Uncle Pete and Auntie Sandra in their front garden, each of them armed with a pair of shears, which they are using to delicately trim the rose bushes that flank their front door. That garden is their pride and joy, especially now that my cousins have grown up and moved out.

Auntie Sandra sees me first and greets me with a smile. "Oh hello, Alex, my love," she says. "Here to see your dad?"

I like Auntie Sandra, but since Mum and Dad split, she always talks to me in this pitying tone of voice, like I'm an abandoned puppy out in a thunderstorm. I know she's just trying to be nice, but it drives me up the wall.

"He's in the annexe," says Uncle Pete, wiping sweat from his forehead with the back of his gardening glove. "But before you go, come here a minute."

I lean my bike against the ivy-strewn wall. I don't really want to go over to Uncle Pete, but I know there's a good chance I'll end up walking away with some money, so I do it.

Uncle Pete pulls off his gloves and winks at me as I approach. Uncle Pete is Dad's older brother and looks like a stretched version of him, taller and thinner. I already know what's going to happen and, sure enough, he pinches my nose between his two fingers, then shoves the tip of his thumb through the middle. "GOT YOUR NOSE!"

I manage a smile because I know what's coming next. He reaches into his back pocket and presses a five pound note into my hand. "Treat yourself to an ice cream, kidder. One for you and one for your girlfriend."

"I haven't got a girlfriend," I grumble.

"I'm not surprised, with that attitude," Uncle Pete chuckles.

What is it with adults and asking if I have a girlfriend? They're obsessed, the lot of them.

I thank Uncle Pete for the money and head through the red wooden gate into the back garden.

Back here, it's even more fancy than the front, with flowers of all different colours, bird baths, a delicately painted shed and even a peeing boy fountain. I walk along the stone path through the lush green lawn until I arrive at the annexe by the back fence.

It's a tiny bungalow with a mossy sloping roof and a sign on the wall that says "Irene's Pad". Sadly, Irene, Auntie Sandra's mum, died about a year ago. Uncle Pete was about to turn it into a "man cave" for himself when Dad showed up, so no one is happy with this new arrangement.

I knock on the door and wait. I can tell it's actually open from the way the door handle is pointing slightly downwards, but I don't want to just walk in. I did that the other day and almost caught Dad naked, about to get in the bath. Don't want that to happen again, thanks very much.

I knock again. One of Dad's peeves at work is people not hearing him when he knocks, so it's funny that he's doing exactly that. I lean over and knock on the window in case the door is too thick to make enough sound.

Nothing. This is weird. I'm going to have to go in. I push the door open.

Inside, the walls are covered in flowery paper and the carpet is thick and spongy. There's a short hallway that leads to a bathroom and tiny bedroom at the end. To the right, through a door, is the lounge and even tinier kitchen all in one.

"Dad?"

No answer.

"DAD?!"

Nothing.

Panic grips my throat. What if he's had an accident? I run along the hall and into the lounge. Oh. Oh no. Dad is sprawled on the floor in front of the TV, which is showing a random YouTube search screen.

"Dad!" I run over and shake him. "Dad, wake up!"

My heart is galloping; my vision is swimming. I've heard about people Dad's age just suddenly dropping dead without warning. Is this what has happened? I try and remember things I've seen in films. How do you check if someone is alive? I press my fingers to his neck, just above the collar of his work shirt. I can feel a pulse. At least I think I can. What if it's just my pulse in my fingers?

"AARGH, THAT'S COLD!"

I scream as Dad suddenly sits up like that wrestler, the Undertaker. His eyes are wild and the hair on the back of his head sticks up like a duck's bum.

"Alex! What are you doing?" he yells.

"What am I doing?" I yell back. "What are *you* doing? I thought you were dead!"

Dad scratches his bristly cheek and blinks hard. "I just dropped off, that's all."

"On the floor?" I say. "What's wrong with the sofa? Or your bed?"

Dad sits cross-legged on the rug and I do the same. It's odd seeing a grown man sitting like a nine-year-old. "If you must know," he says, "I was doing a workout."

I splutter with laughter. I can't help it. Dad doesn't see the funny side, though.

"All right," he says. "See if you're still laughing when you're my age and you can't eat all the burgers and ice cream you want without turning into the Blob." He pats his belly, which continues to jiggle for a couple of seconds afterwards.

"So you fell asleep halfway through a workout?" I say.

Dad sighs. "They tell you to rest for a minute between exercises. I closed my eyes and, well, the next thing I knew you were about to wheel me off to the morgue."

Dad stands up, familiar firework display noises of groans, cracks and pops coming from his body. "So what brings you down to the shed this evening?"

Dad always calls his flat a shed. "Had my own house and now I live in my brother's shed." Stuff like that. I get up and face him.

"I wanted to see how much you'd managed to write," I say.

Dad looks at the floor again and his face goes a little pink. "Um, well, you know," he says, scratching the back of his head. "Just mainly been in the plotting stage."

"OK," I say, trying not to feel too disappointed. "So, what have you been plotting?"

Dad shifts from foot to foot. "Oh, you know," he says. "Characters. Storylines … plot twists."

I close my eyes. "You haven't started it, have you?"

Dad lets out a slow, slow breath. "No."

"Why not?" I can sense my hope for our family falling away from me already.

Dad chuckles. "This is all backwards. It should be me hassling you about not doing your homework."

"Well, a lot of things should be a certain way, but they aren't," I snap. "We're living in Backwards World, aren't we?"

Dad plonks himself down on the sofa, sending the doily on the back sliding off behind. "I'm just tired, son. You know how it is. By the time I'm done with work, I want to sit down and write, but it's like wading through treacle. I started off really positively. I went for a run and everything."

"A run?" I say, almost gasping.

He nods. "It was a bad idea. You see, the thing is, my spirit is willing but my body." He lifts his arm and lets it flop back down on to a sofa cushion. "It's not the fine-tuned machine it once was." He stops and rubs his eyes. "I just need a holiday, I think."

A lump starts to form in my throat, but it's instantly dissolved by an idea. Well, calling it an idea would be overplaying it. It's half an idea. Maybe a quarter. But it might be something.

"So you're saying if you didn't have work, you'd be able to get the book written?"

"Definitely," he replies. "But it's not like I can just not turn up to work, is it?"

I rub my chin. "Of course it isn't," I say. "That would be silly."

Chapter Four

I've spent hours trying to make the website look official. I copied the Post UK logo, found what font they used, everything. I found a service that lets you make a webpage for free and put it on there. I grabbed a couple of photos online of the Post UK boss shaking hands with people and smiling. Maybe this is just my tiredness talking, but I think it looks convincing.

Then, after I did that, I had to create a letter. I found an old work letter of Dad's in a drawer and copied the exact layout. It took me ages to get the words right, but it's finally done. Man, it's gone eleven o'clock.

And I know this isn't the Natural Order of Things. In fact, it's about as far away from that as you can get. But right now, I'm willing to try anything to get it back, and if this works, it will all be worth it.

I'm in the spare room. Dad designated it as his office, but it's really more of a dumping ground. It bothers me, knowing it's there, all disorganized and untidy. I want it to be like my room – ordered, straight, everything in its right place – but I don't even know where to start.

Right now, though, that's not important. What is important is that this is the room with a printer in it.

I just checked and it looks like Mum is fast asleep in her room at the other end of the landing. Everything sounds quiet in Indie's room too. Time to initiate OPERATION PRINT THE FAKE LETTER.

My first attempt at printing gives me a blank page.

My second has lines all through it. Nowhere near official-looking enough. That's when a red light starts flashing, "Change printer ink".

I growl under my breath. Now I see why Dad was always yelling at this thing.

I know Dad used to keep spare ink cartridges

somewhere in the spare room, but not where exactly. Dad's not one of those people who has a system for things. He just throws things anywhere and hopes for the best. I try the drawers under the window, but there is nothing but ancient letters and a couple of Dad's darts trophies.

There's a pile of three boxes near the door. Maybe there'll be some in one of those. I carefully remove the top box and place it on the floor. Nothing in there but junk, by the looks of things: a couple of screwdrivers, some electrical cables for stuff that was probably thrown out years ago, a tie, a wrestling figure … but then I see a thick brown book, buried at the bottom of the box. I don't remember seeing it before, or maybe I have but wasn't paying any attention. Either way, it has my interest now.

I pull it out and wipe a film of dust away with the bottom of my T-shirt. It smells musty, like the back corner of a library. I open it up and inside are loads of photos of Mum and Dad together. At the beginning they don't look much older than Indie; they have weird hair and Dad's wearing a track suit that makes me seasick just looking at it, but they're so happy. Mum's head is resting on Dad's shoulder and they both have their eyes closed and mouths open, like they're laughing. The photo couldn't have been posed. Someone must have snapped them sharing a little joke. How could so much go so wrong?

"What are you doing?"

I shriek like I've shut my finger in a car door and throw the book down.

"Ever heard of knocking?" I huff.

"On the spare room door?" Indie says, her arms folded.

My heart is hammering like it's about to explode. She must have crept out of her room like a ninja in black pyjamas.

Indie steps into the room, reaches past me and picks up the book. She takes a look but doesn't seem to find it as emotional as I do.

Throwing it back in the box, she blows out through her lips. "That's ancient history. You might as well read *Beowulf.*"

"Bear what?" I say.

Indie rolls her eyes. "You're such an ignoramus, Alex. Look, if you want my advice—"

"I don't," I cut in.

"Well, I'm going to give it to you because, unbelievably, I am your older sister and that's my job."

"Fine." I sigh.

"You need to leave that Mum and Dad stuff where it belongs." She pointed at the photo album. "In the past."

"But—"

This time she interrupted me. "You need to move on to the acceptance phase like I have. Accept that it's a lost cause and move on with your life."

My skin goes prickly. I want to explode at her. How can she give up so easily? But I know if I do that, I risk giving away the plan before it's even started. Keep your cool, Alex.

"I wasn't even looking at that, so your speech was a total waste of time," I say, trying to sound convincing. "I was looking for printer cartridges, if you must know."

"They're in the drawer where they always are," says Indie.

"No they're not. I checked."

Indie sighs deeply and stomps over to the drawers. That's her all over: never takes my word for anything. Always has to see for herself.

"Ta da!" she says sarcastically, holding up the box of cartridges. "Try moving things if you want to find them."

I grumble under my breath. Mum always says the same thing and it's so annoying.

"What are you printing, anyway?"

"Homework," I blurt, about a millisecond after she asked. It was an excuse I had prepared beforehand, but judging by Indie's reaction, I think I rushed it. The sad fact is she knows me. She knows me better than anyone. And I hate it.

"Don't buy it," she says. "Not even you do homework this early in the summer holidays."

It's only now I remember the laptop on the desk, complete with Dad's fake letter and fake website on the screen. If I make a quick run and slam the lid down, she'll get suspicious. I need to think of something more subtle.

"Look at the size of that spider above the door!"

"Where?" Indie yelps.

As soon as she spins around, I take a couple of hops across the room and quickly minimize the windows.

"I can't see a spider!" she says.

"Oh, I think it ran behind that unit," I say, but

Indie's giving me that look with her arms folded that she always does.

"I saw you get rid of that window."

Oh bum.

"No you didn't."

"What is it? A love letter to your secret crush?" she coos.

"Shut up, Indie," I warn.

"Which one is she? Is she that girl who hangs around outside the chippy growling at people? Or the one who walks past our house singing Taylor Swift every day? Oh my God, it's one of the dinner ladies, isn't it?"

"It's not a love letter," I snap.

"Well, you're up to something, Ally boy," she says.

"Am not."

She doesn't even acknowledge my denial. "I can tell when you're plotting, Alex. You go all quiet; you shut yourself away; you get even more obsessively organized. Don't think I didn't notice the cutlery drawer had been re-stacked this morning."

"Well, it was high time," I say. "Small spoons and big spoons should be in separate areas. Separate!"

"Whatever," says Indie, waving me off. "Just

keep whatever you're doing down, OK? I'm trying to work on a sonnet in there."

I wait until she's gone and I can hear the customary noisy clatter of her typewriter in her bedroom before barricading the door shut, replacing the ink cartridges and printing the letter.

It looks amazing. Really genuine.

I can't wait until all this pays off and I can laugh right in Indie's face. How about THAT for a lost cause?

OPERATION PRINT THE FAKE
LETTER: COMPLETE

Chapter Five

Dad's lips move as he reads the letter, his forehead creased. All I can hear is my pulse thudding in my head.

I hardly slept last night thinking about this moment. I went backwards and forwards between "he'll buy it" and "there's no way, not in a billion years", over and over, but I knew I had to at least try.

Dad puts the letter down on the granny coffee table and sits with his elbows on his knees, his hands forming a canopy on which to rest his head. I try and read his expression, figure out what he's going to say, but he just looks confused. After what feels like a dog year, he opens his mouth and finally speaks.

"This is unbelievable, son," he says.

Hang on a second. Does he mean unbelievable like "good", or unbelievable like "actually unbelievable"? As in he doesn't believe it?

"I, um, thought you'd be pleased," I say, trying desperately to stop my voice from wobbling.

Dad looks at me, but I can't keep eye contact, so I focus on an ornament of an old shepherd leaning on his stick next to a headless sheep. I'm guessing that was broken off at some point because, if not, that's a really disturbing design.

"I am pleased, Alex, I just..." Dad stops and shakes his head. "Run it by me again."

I take a deep breath. It was bad enough going through my prepared speech once, let alone twice.

"OK, so I knew you wanted to write a book but your job made you too tired," I say. "So I checked with your work and they were running this really exclusive scheme where they let you have a summer off, fully paid, but you have to produce something by the end of it."

"I've never heard of this scheme before," Dad says.

"It wasn't very well advertised," I say. "But look, there's a website!"

I get my phone out and show him.

POST UK ARTISTIC LEAVE SCHEME

Underneath the photos of random people shaking hands with the CEO, I added some fake names. "Fred Belcher accepts his place on last year's scheme." Stuff like that.

Dad frowns at the screen, his lips moving slightly as he reads. Then he looks back at me really intensely, like he's trying to read my thoughts. "But you applied *for* me?" he says. "Why didn't you just tell me about it?"

I shrug. "There's a lot of stuff going on. I thought you wouldn't get around to it."

Dad shakes his head and puffs out his cheeks. "I don't know what to say, son. This is amazing."

He's going for it. He's really going for it. The letter and the website were the perfect double whammy!

"I get four weeks off work? Paid?"

I nod. "But you have to write your book."

Dad chuckles. "This is exactly what I needed. A real kick up the backside. I should probably call Peregrine, though. Make sure it's all sorted."

"It is!" I blurt so loud, Dad's hand stops halfway to his pocket. "I spoke to him myself. He said not to call."

"Really?" says Dad.

"Yeah!" I nod so hard my head's in danger of coming loose. "In fact, one of the terms of the scheme is that you're not allowed to have contact with work at all. Under no circumstances."

"Oh," says Dad. "Well, makes sense, I suppose. To make sure people are left alone properly to do their creative work."

I point at him, grinning big. "I bet that's what it is!"

That's a pretty good idea to come up with just like that. Not bad.

My heart is turning cartwheels! You've done it, Alex! You're a genius!

OPERATION CONVINCE DAD
NOT TO GO TO WORK SO HE CAN
WRITE HIS BOOK: COMPLETE

Chapter Six

It's Monday morning, 5.57 a.m. precisely, and I'm standing outside the door of the depot. The radio is already on and I can hear Lloyd and Miriam inside setting up. I scoped out the car park for Peregrine's massive motor, but thankfully it's not here.

5.58. Dad officially starts at six. I don't want to be late. But I can't do this. To be honest, I've been so focused on Dad, I haven't thought much about this next bit. But now it's pretty obvious it's going to be the hardest part.

Come on, you convinced Dad. How hard can Lloyd and Miriam be?

I take a breath, count down from ten and walk inside.

Miriam does a double take when she sees me.

Obviously, I don't have a uniform, so I'm wearing the closest I could find: grey shorts and a red T-shirt. I laid them out last night so I could stay as long as possible in bed. I was up so early, Mum and Indie have no idea I've even left my bedroom

"Alex?" says Miriam. "What are you doing here? And where's your dad?"

Lloyd chuckles through a mouthful of toast. "That is Carl, Mizzer. He's just been using that anti-aging cream."

"Actually, Dad's going to be off for the next four weeks," I say, my voice doing that annoying up and down thing again.

Miriam and Lloyd look at me like I've just told them I'm actually a lizard.

"How's he managed that?" asks Lloyd. "Won the lottery?"

"It's a, um, scheme," I say, cringing a little at the double meaning I've just noticed.

"What scheme is this?" asks Miriam, looking a little envious.

"It's with school," I say. "I have to do Dad's job for the summer. It's like a work experience thing. Look, I have a letter!"

I pass them a letter I made last night. This

time, it has my school's logo on it. I hope it seems convincing to them because right now I feel like the worst lying liar who ever lied.

They read the letter together, Lloyd tapping at the edge of it with the stump of his finger. After what feels like a century, he hands it back.

"Very nice," says Lloyd. "But can't you do mine instead?"

"I've never heard of that scheme," says Miriam. She's fully turned around and is looking at me with her arms folded. I stare at a poster on the wall behind her. "AVOID DOG BITES," it reads.

"It's a new thing," I say. "Like a trial run."

Miriam stares at me just like Dad did when I told him. I'm too uncomfortable to look back, so I focus on a crack in the wall behind her.

"How come your dad never said anything to us about it?" she asks.

How did I not think of that? Of course it is exactly the kind of thing you would tell them about. Having four weeks off and getting your son to replace you isn't exactly everyday stuff, is it?

"Well," I say, "he was, um, supposed to be with me today, to train me, but he's sick. Dodgy kebab last night."

Miriam stares at me a little longer, then her mouth turns down at the corners and her eyebrows shoot up. "OK. Well, I suppose that means it's up to us to train you?"

"Um, yeah, I guess?" I say.

Lloyd rubs his hands together. "Great. Let's brainwash this youngster in the ways of the Fishwick posties."

Dad always says he hates Mondays. For some reason, it's always busy. Tuesdays are always a breeze: there are hardly any letters, a few parcels and the bags are nice and light. Wednesdays are even worse than Mondays, but at least by then, he says, you're into the week a little bit more.

Each round has a fitting, with slots for each house and a desk underneath. All three desks have two plastic boxes full of letters. Against Lloyd's fitting, there are at least ten huge grey sacks, bursting with parcels. Lloyd and Miriam scoop up one each and tip them upside down on to the grotty rug in the middle of the room, sending the packages spilling everywhere. Seeing it makes my teeth itch. Surely there's a more organized way of doing this? Something less messy?

"All right, Alex, you can start by digging in,"

says Lloyd, nodding at the mountain. "All you've got to do is chuck them on the right fitting. Even a monkey could do it. Just look at Miriam." Miriam responds by firing a box at his head.

I watch what the other two do. They scoop up a parcel and after a half-second glance at the label, throw it at one of the three fittings. I have to dodge a couple of boxes flying my way already.

I pick up a parcel. Kingfisher Close. Where's that? I turn and look at my fitting. All the streets have their own colour: Jepsom Street is blue, Kelly Drive is red, Green Avenue is black, which is really annoying. I can't see Kingfisher Close, though.

"What? You lost, kidder?" says Miriam, while chucking two parcels in two different directions.

"Kingfisher Close," I say.

She nods at Lloyd. "Kingfisher over there."

"Anything that sounds like a bird is mine," says Lloyd, digging into the pile. "Kestrel, Sparrowhawk, Eagle, you get the idea."

That seems easy enough. I pick up another. Phoenix House. Good. Another bird. I throw it over to Lloyd's fitting. While he picks up another load, he glances at it resting on his desk.

"That's yours, mate," he says, lobbing it back with his spare hand.

"But I thought you had the birds," I say.

"Real birds, not mythical ones."

And it goes on like that, with Lloyd and Miriam doing most of the work and me sorting the odd one, mainly by squinting at the street names on the other fittings. When we're finally all sorted, each fitting has a huge pile of parcels on it. And it looks like mine is the biggest.

Lloyd stands back and looks, hands on hips. "That one always gets loads."

Lucky me!

"Here, I'll show you how to chuck it up," he says, obviously sensing that I don't know where to begin.

Lloyd clears a path on the desk with his four-and-a-half-fingered hand and grabs a wodge of mail from one of the boxes.

"This is the easy bit," he says. "This mail will all be in sequence. All you do is whack it in the slot. A donkey could do it. Just look at Miriam."

Lloyd passes me a handful of letters and points to where I start. He is way quicker than me and keeps catching me up, picking up more letters and overtaking me.

"That's it, lad," he says. "Easy, isn't it?"

It is. It's also kind of boring. I can see why Dad's so miserable having to get up at six and do this every day.

"Now on to these suckers," says Lloyd, slapping his hand down on a big box with "FRAGILE" on it. "You're going to want to put these up there." He nods at some shelves above the fitting. There are five of them, separated by dividers. I recognize Dad's handwriting in marker pen on each of them: **BAG 1-2**, **BAG 3-4**, **BAG 5-6**, **BAG 7-8**, **BAG 9-10**. That's when I notice more of Dad's scrawling on the fitting itself, numbers one to ten dotted across the frame in order.

"So you're going to want to see which bag the parcel goes in and throw it on that shelf. Now, us lot have been doing it for years and know who the usual suspects are, but you're not going to have a scooby, so when you get a parcel for somewhere, just flip any letters for that address so they are facing the other way. Then, when you get to it, you'll know to look for one."

Lloyd picks up a parcel and gently pats the address label with his half-finger. "Six Jubilee Street." Then he reaches across to the slot for that address, pulls out the letters and, with a quick flick of his wrist, turns them around and puts them back in. Then he throws them on to the shelf that says, "**BAG 5-6**."

"Another thing to look out for," he says, pointing at a sticker with a paw on it next to a slot. "This means they've got a dog. Now you've got to be extra careful there." He turns and calls over his shoulder. "Hey, Mizzer, what's the number one thing people say when their dog comes running over to you?"

"Oh, he's all right, he won't hurt you!" Miriam replies, without missing a beat.

"And what do they always do?" says Lloyd.

"Hurt you," Miriam fires back.

Lloyd raises his eyebrows at me, so high they touch the lip of his black bandana. "And make sure not to stick your fingers through the letter boxes too far," he says, resting his half-finger on my shoulder. "Or you might live to regret it."

I glance down at the finger. This one seems more plausible than his usual stories.

"Any questions?" he says.

About a million, the first one being, "Can I really do this?" and the second one being, "No, but seriously, can I?"

I glance up at the mountain of parcels. Will I really get them all delivered? Will I be out when it's still dark, using the torch on my phone to read envelopes? Will I get lost? But there are no questions I can really put to Lloyd without him suspecting something, so I shake my head.

"Righty ho," he says, with a wink. "Well, if you need help just give me or Miriam a shout. Actually, best to avoid Miriam. She's always grumpy before she's had her fifth coffee of the day."

"I heard that, you cheeky old beggar," says Miriam, without turning around.

"See what I mean?" Lloyd whispers.

When I'm sorting on my own, it's not too bad, but I'm slower than Lloyd and Miriam. They pick up a parcel and it's in the right place in half a second, while I have to stand and stare at the frame until I see the street name and number. By the time I'm done, Lloyd and Miriam are bagged up and ready to go.

"See? Told you it was easy," says Lloyd.

"Am I done now?"

Lloyd chuckles. "Not quite. You done your redirections?"

"My redi-what?"

Lloyd laughs and ruffles my hair. "And I can see you haven't done your leaflets."

"I have leaflets?"

Lloyd goes to the corner of the room and comes back with two stacks of brightly coloured glossy paper, bound with white plastic strapping.

"It's got to go to every address, but you get all week to deliver it," he says. "This week we've got pizzas and funerals."

"Nice combination," I say.

"Well, if the pizza poisons you, at least your burial will be reasonable," says Lloyd before turning to Miriam, who's halfway out of the door with two rammed post bags. "Start doing young Alex's leaflets, will you?"

Miriam groans. "But I hate doing those things!"

"Don't we all?" says Lloyd. "But we need to help the young whippersnapper out. We were all new once. Mind you, back when you started, the stamps had Richard the Third on them."

"If my arms weren't full, I'd whack you," says Miriam.

So after throwing her bags in the van, Miriam shoves a load of pizza and funeral leaflets into half the slots on my frame while Lloyd shows me how to do redirections. It's just a thing for people who move house: if a letter is addressed to the name of someone who has moved out, you put on a sticker for their new house.

"OK, so now you're ready to band up," says Lloyd. "Bundle up the mail, stick a couple of elastic bands on, shove them in a bag with the parcels, then chuck the bags in your trolley. Bish, bash, bosh, job's a good'un. You going to be all right? I'm sure your old man showed you that at least?"

"Yeah, of course he did," I say.

"Good," says Lloyd. "Well, we'd better go. If we stay in one place too long, Peregrine will get annoyed." He waves his scanner. "See you later, kid. Have a good day!"

And with that, Lloyd and Miriam get in their van and leave. I glance at the grimy clock on the wall. It's nine thirty. I'll be out of here by ten, no problem.

Chapter Seven

How is it nearly eleven o'clock?

My hands are sore from these INFURIATING elastic bands snapping every time I try to bundle up some mail. All the bags are in the trolley, but there's so much stuff the lid won't close properly. If Mum and Dad aren't back together by the end of this, I am going to be furious.

Groaning with the strain, I force the trolley out of the depot, down the bumpy track, and on to the High Street. To get to my first bit, I have to walk up a hill. There is no way around it. I lean over until I'm almost bent double as I push. My legs burn with the effort. A man with a pushchair overtakes me. As does an old lady with a tartan shopping trolley. The sun peeps from behind the cloud and soon sweat is running into my eyes, making them sting. It's only when I reach the top of the hill I realize I've forgotten my scanner. I groan the kind of word I really shouldn't be saying. A lady watering her roses tuts. I leave the trolley and run back down the hill, scoop up the scanner from the depot, then begin the trek back up. At least it's easier without an eighteen-tonne trolley to heave.

My heart drops and my stomach twists. The trolley is gone! No. No, no, no, this can't be happening. Lloyd had specifically told me to chain it to a lamp post so no one steals it, but I was only gone a minute. Two, tops. I think I'm going to cry.

What am I going to do? Think logically, Alex. Maybe no one will miss their stuff? Maybe I'll get away with it. But what about the trolley? How am I going to explain that? Oh, I'm finished. This whole plan is over before it's even started.

"Excuse me, postie!"

I wheel around to seek out the source of the voice. On the other side of the road, standing in front of a house covered in Christmas lights, is a man in a light-up Rudolph jumper. And he has my trolley.

"Merry Christmas!" he yells.

It's August, but whatever. I'm so relieved I haven't lost everything that I go along with it.

"I just thought I'd put it on my drive while you went back, just to be on the safe side," the man says. "There are some dodgy characters about."

I take another look at him. He's about my granddad's age, with hair poking out of his nose and ears. Perched atop his bald head is a pair of flashing antlers. I remember Dad mentioning him before: "Christmas Mick". Celebrates Christmas all year round. Dad always moaned about all the stuff Christmas Mick had delivered, but receiving Christmas tips in the summer was always a nice bonus.

"So you're the new postie, are you?" says Christmas Mick, the red nose on his jumper winking weakly.

"For a little while," I say. That is if I haven't died of a heart attack because you've stolen my trolley again, you big Christmassy weirdo.

Christmas Mick chuckles and shakes his head, making the antlers wobble. "They get younger and younger. What happened to Carl? Is he off gallivanting?"

"Something like that," I say, crossing the road

and standing on the path in front of his drive. "Can I have my trolley back, please?"

"Of course!" Christmas Mick pushes the trolley towards me. I grab the handle and apply the brake before it rolls all the way back down the hill. "I mustn't delay you any further. That would be like stopping Santa's sleigh on Christmas Eve!"

"Right," I say, heaving the trolley away. "Thanks for looking after it, then!"

The trolley seems to be even heavier this time around. I remember the first house in bag one was 180 Sunset Hill, so I stop the trolley next to a lamp post outside there and secure it with the bike lock.

I find bag one and sling it across my shoulder. Ouch. That is heavy. No wonder Dad is always moaning about his bad back. I drag the first bundle of mail out and carefully remove the bands in case they twang off and take my eyes out. Here we go: two letters for 180. I walk up the drive, lift the flap and post it. Easy! One down, about six hundred and fifty to go!

When I get to the end of the drive, I see the next house is 178, which is the next one down. I groan. I'm going to have to climb the hill again, aren't I? How does Dad do this every day? Suddenly, him falling asleep on the floor is beginning to make sense.

Halfway down the hill, I see the letter for 148 is turned around. That means they must have a parcel. I try a pretty big cardboard box, but it's not that one. Then I try what feels like a dress in plastic wrapping. Not that one either. I dig deeper with one hand, gripping the bundle of mail with the other. I can feel something right at the bottom, but I can't get it. There's too much stuff on top of it. "Come on, you silly—"

PFFFFFFFFFFFFFTTTTTPLPLPLPL

Oh noooo. No, no, no. I was concentrating so hard on grabbing the parcel, I must have loosened my grip on the mail, because now it's all over the floor. I haul the back-shattering bag off and drop it with a thud that sounds like someone falling out of a tree, sit on the path and start trying to put the letters back in order. Oh, and what's that? Great. It's raining.

Carl woke up at five, even without his alarm. He tried to have a lie-in, but after years of the same routine, his body was trained to wake at that time and wouldn't allow him to go back to sleep.

He padded into the lounge in his dressing gown and slippers, a steaming mug of tea in his hand. It felt strange to be here at this time. He should be at work, listening to Lloyd and Miriam arguing while the radio droned in the background.

He slumped on the old sofa, which creaked under his weight and took a deep breath, imagining the long, luxurious summer stretched out in front of him like a white sand tropical beach.

He was about to turn on the TV, like he always did when he sat down, but he stopped. The laptop sat on the table by the window, illuminated by a beam of early morning light.

Of course, he didn't have the summer off. Not really. He was going to have to work. Work harder than he'd ever done before. This was his chance to finally make something of his life. To have a career to be proud of. To show Kate he was worth another chance.

Carl stood up, ignoring the sound of his cracking knees and hips, and went over to the table. He sat down and opened it up. He had forgotten about this laptop. When he'd given up on his most recent attempt at a book, he'd passed the computer to Alex, who eventually got a better one. Carl assumed this one had been thrown out, but here it was. And on the desktop, hidden behind rows of icons, was a photo of the family. The four of them standing in front of a waterfall on holiday. They were all in their swimming costumes and they were smiling, even Alex, who was wary about the slippery rocks and cold water. That had been a great day.

Carl felt that familiar boulder of grief form in his throat, so he quickly clicked on the word processor, which blocked the picture with white blankness. Sometimes things are so beautiful, it hurts to look at them. *Wait a second, that's a pretty good line,* Carl thought. Better write it down. First, time to find that old story he started all those years ago.

He scrolled down the document box, past a load of Alex's homework assignments, until he found what he was looking for: *The Last Letter.* He noticed the date it was last opened. Four years ago. Wow. That long?

Carl clicked on the file and waited for it to load. There were only three thousand words in the word count tally in the taskbar at the bottom, but the rest would surely arrive soon. It was an old file and the computer hadn't been used in an age; surely some warming up was required.

He waited.

And waited.

But three thousand words was all there was.

Carl frantically scrolled up and down, thinking it must be some kind of mistake, but no, that was all he had written.

Carl took a swig from his tea, but it was still too hot and his mouth was on fire. How could it only be three thousand words? In his memory, he had worked on this for months. It was epic. Not perfect, of course, but surely there was more to it than *this*?

Carl scrolled down to the last paragraph he had written and groaned out loud. This was bad. This was really bad.

The postman opened the door of the cottage and found old Mrs Bloom lying at the bottom of the stairs. He checked her vitals, but it was obvious from the coldness of her skin that she was long gone. Poor old lady. This was no way to go. But wait a second. Is that a gun on the floor? WHY WOULD THE MURDERER LEAVE THE WEAPON AT THE SCENE, CARL? THAT'S SO STUPID. I CAN'T DO THIS I CAN'T DO THIS I CAN'T DO THIS...

And it went on like that. In fact, without the rows of repeated "I CAN'T DO THIS", it would only be two and a half thousand words.

Carl rubbed his eyes and clicked "New". He was going to have to start from scratch.

Chapter Eight

Dad is supposed to finish at two o'clock. It is now three o'clock and I am only on bag six. I still have four more after this. That first bag took me an hour. Mostly because I had to put all the letters back together, but also because all the ones that were flipped were now no longer flipped, and I forgot where all my parcels were. So when I got back to the trolley, I still had three in there, which – guess what? – meant another trip down and up the hill.

Oh, and here's another problem: the scanner. Turns out you have to log in. Luckily, Dad is very predictable and uses the same PIN for everything (5762), so I could get in pretty easily, but this thing is way more complicated than I was expecting. There's all these different functions: Deliver to

Customer, Deliver to Neighbour, Safe Place, Not Delivered, and then the option to input the reason it's not delivered. And do you think these things work in the rain? I stood there outside a house trying to deliver a parcel, jabbing at it for ages, while getting absolutely drenched. And writing out one of those cards when they're turning into papier-mâché in your hand? Nightmare! And then when you've finally written out the card and they decide to answer the door? AAAARRRGGHHH!

The rain has stopped now, but my clothes are all soaked and stuck to my body, and the cold wind is making me shiver. I thought it was supposed to be summer.

I hoist the next bag on to my shoulder and wince at the pain. Can I keep this up for four whole weeks?

If my plan works, it will all be worth it.

I cross the humpbacked bridge over the canal. Glancing down, I see that *Lola* boat still moored. The red-haired girl whose pale face I saw scowling out of the shutters is sitting on the roof, cross-legged, dangling a piece of string in front of the black cat I nearly ran over. Even from here, I can see the look of intense concentration on her face.

Can you even train a cat? It's not like they'll let you tame them, is it? It's only when her eyes snap up to the bridge that I realize I'm staring at her. I try and make it look like I was just appreciating the canal and carry on quickly.

I've got letters for Fairbirch House, and I have no idea where that is. I check the house further up and that's 142. Who gives houses names, anyway? They're not pets. Absolute nonsense.

Hold on, there's a dirt track just up ahead on the right. There are tall trees standing either side, but I can see a house at the end of it. Looks big. Maybe that's it.

When I get to the top of the drive, I find a pretty snooty-looking house: grand wooden front door, fountain of a naked lady pouring water, and a plaque on the wall that reads "Fairbirch House". Well, of course it is.

When I get to the door, I find it has one of those really old-fashioned letter boxes that are only just wide enough to get a postcard through. Problem is, their letters are thick, A4-sized things and I have to fold them in half and force them through one at a time. I'm just posting the first one when,

WRRRRRAAAWWWWW!

There's a scream on the other side of the door and the letter is yanked inside. I let out a little cry of surprise. I can't help it. What the heck was that?

The letter box flap opens from the other side and a pair of eyes glare back. Oh my God. This house looks really old – it might be a ghost! I turn and make a run for it, but—

SPLOOOOOSH!

What? Huh? I look down and I'm ankle-deep in water. I've run into the fountain. Wow. Why make a fountain so low people can just step into it? A health and safety hazard. That's what it is.

"Oi!"

I turn around and the front door is open. But it's not a ghost. It's even worse than that. Swaggering towards me are Holden Jones and Greg Tripps, the two biggest bullies in my year. Scratch that, the entire school. The kind of kids who think it's funny to suddenly make loud noises at you in the corridor then laugh when you flinch. WELL OF COURSE I FLINCHED, IT'S EVOLUTIONARY INSTINCT!

"Why you standing in my fountain?" asks Holden.

"And why are you a postman?" adds Greg.

"Both valid questions," I say. "But I'm in a hurry, so…" I hop out of the fountain, slip on the step, just about managing to stay upright.

"Seriously, though, Alex," says Holden. "What's going on? I mean, I knew you were weird, but cosplaying as Postman Pat and splashing around in a fountain is a whole new level."

My face burns. Since when did Holden Jones live in Fishwick? In a mansion? Life is *so* not fair.

"What you got in your bag?" asks Greg, rubbing his chin like the supervillain he's clearly in training to be.

I shrug. "Letters," I mumble.

"That bag is sick, man," says Holden. "Can I have it?" He says it like it's not a question, voice flat, eyes dead.

"No, it's not mine," I say, taking a couple of steps back.

"Then you won't mind me having it, then," says Holden, keeping up with me, Greg in tow.

I know how this goes. I know how it always goes. It's as predictable as a quadratic equation: they're going to steal the bag.

I can't let them. I take off down the drive, my squelchy shoes slipping in the rain-sodden mud.

I hear them behind me, panting and yelling and hooting. If I can reach the main road, maybe they'll leave me alone.

They don't leave me alone. Greg catches up and grips my bag with a meaty hand and I'm dragged backwards, the strap cutting into my neck. A car comes down the road. Surely they'll stop and help me.

They don't.

The strap drags up my neck and on to my face, rubbing and burning. I'm going to have to let it go. Holden joins in and pulls.

CLOMP.

The strap snaps and it hits the floor, sending parcels and mail bundles spilling everywhere. Holden scoops up a bundle and Greg grabs a parcel with "FRAGILE" written on it.

"Give them back!" I yell, but my voice comes out all strangled and it makes them laugh even more.

"Give them back, give them back!" Holden crows.

I chase them up the street. It's a dead end, leading to just one old house, all broken down and ramshackle. I doubt anyone even lives there.

Holden and Greg stop outside the house, still

laughing. I can't let them keep those. I remember Dad telling me about when Lloyd got robbed years ago. There was a big investigation and at one point they were questioning Lloyd as if he was in on it. What will I do if that happens? I'm not even supposed to be working here!

"You're going to have to beg for it," says Holden.

"Come on, Holden," I moan. "Why are you doing this?"

"Why do you care, man?" says Greg. "Like, how are you a postman?"

"I'm just helping my dad, all right?" I say.

Holden laughs. "So our regular postman is *your dad*? Yeah, I can see the resemblance. Both butt ugly."

Greg, who is probably getting bored, slams the parcel on the ground. I hear it smash. "Here, you can have that one back," he says, and kicks it in my direction, destroying it even more.

"Now can I have the letters?" I say. "Please."

"Like I said, you'll have to beg," says Holden.

I groan. "Please."

"You'll have to do better than that."

"Please, Holden, please."

Holden laughs. "On your knees."

I look at Greg, hoping that he'll have mercy on me and call Holden off, but there is no mercy in his piggy little eyes.

"Knees."

Looks like I have no choice. My knees hit the wet floor, sending the two apes into hysterics.

"I can't believe he's actually done it," Greg booms.

"Can you give it back now?" I say.

Holden chuckles and throws the bundle to Greg. Then Greg throws it back. "Go long!" says Holden.

They're not going to give it back, are they?

BANG BANG BANG BANG BANG!

Behind them, a rickety gate flies open and a lady who looks about a hundred stomps out, clattering a metal spoon against a frying pan.

"Leave him alone, you little grot bags!" she screeches, coming after them, still banging.

Holden throws his hands up, dropping the bundle.

"I know your mother!" she yells. "And if I see either of you around here again, I'll give you both a thick ear."

Her threat seems to work, because they slope off

back down the road towards his house. I pick up the bundle, which at least has stayed intact, along with the parcel, which sounds like it's in a million pieces.

The old lady looks at me, her chin jutting out and her gums exposed. "You all right, my love?"

I nod and try to stop the embarrassed tears from coming.

"You're Carl's boy, aren't you?" she says.

She must clock that I look surprised because she explains, "I've seen you out with him before. My chair's by the window, you see. I don't miss a thing." She peers up at the sky through thick glasses. "Looks like it's going to rain again. Wait there."

With that, she turns and hobbles back through the gate. I should probably do as she says; she's scary. She returns a minute later with a long blue raincoat with a hood. It looks dorky as heck, but I'll take anything I can get.

"Here you go, darling," she says. "It don't look much, but it'll protect you from the elements."

"Oh, thanks," I say.

"You can keep it, I've no use for it," she says. "My name's Brenda."

I remember Dad talking about her. Usually

followed by something like, "she's batty but harmless." I don't know about harmless. I think she was ready to harm Holden and Greg.

A raindrop splats on my head. Time to put on the coat. Thanks, Brenda.

Chapter Nine

I finally post my last letter at five o'clock. After dropping off my trolley at the depot, I arrive home just before Mum. I peel off my sodden clothes and jump in the shower, then lie down on my bed, only to be awoken what feels like five seconds later by a shout from downstairs.

"Alex, dinner!"

The smell of cooking wafts up the stairs and I don't even know what it is, but I'm so starving I could eat a diseased goat.

I get up, make my bed so it's not creased and head downstairs. I find Mum and Indie at the table, three plates piled high with chilli and rice. Not my favourite, but it'll do.

I sit down and immediately shove a forkful into

my face. It's too hot and it hurts my mouth, but I tough through it.

"Someone's hungry," Mum chuckles.

"You've been out all day, Alex," says Indie, peering at me over her phone. "What have you been up to?"

"Just been out on a bike ride," I say.

"All day?" says Mum. "Where did you bike to? Paris?"

"I'm telling you," says Indie. "He's up to something. I mean, did you see that mystery coat hanging up in the hall?"

I internally curse myself for not hiding Brenda's raincoat.

"I'm not up to anything. Shut up, Indie," I say, my mouth full of chilli again. "It's just my friend's coat. I'm borrowing it."

Indie honks with laughter. "That Spencer gonk is in France, remember? Since when do you have other friends?"

"I've got loads," I grumble through gritted teeth.

She needs to drop this, because I do not have the energy to defend myself. I don't really have the energy for anything.

"I think it's a girl," says Indie. "It looks like a girl's coat for one thing."

I groan. "Shut. Up."

"Ooooooh, that's so sweet," Mum coos. "What's her name?"

"There is no girl," I say. "I was just out on a bike ride."

Mum and Indie laugh. I hate being the only boy in the house so much, I can't even begin to explain. When she goes off to uni next year, it will be a big relief.

"Well, I bet you'll go on a bike ride tomorrow too," says Indie.

My heart sinks. I've got to do all that again, haven't I? In those minutes after waking up, I somehow forgot.

"None of your business," I mumble.

Obviously, that does nothing to shut them up, and I polish off the rest of dinner in silence and then immediately go back to bed.

The Badlands

Carlos cranked the handle on his Harley and took off across the Badlands, kicking up orange dust into the parched desert air.

As the wind blew through his flowing mane, Carlos surveyed his turf. He knew every cactus, every bumpy side track, every lizard that scuttled between rocks in the heat of the midday sun. He had worked out here all his adult life, delivering letters to the residents of the Badlands scattered across the bleak landscape like pebbles cast into a wishing well.

There was Mick who celebrated Christmas all year round, and Brenda, the antiques expert whose trailer was crammed from floor to ceiling with knick-knacks and doodahs. There was Babs, the friendly street mutt and many more besides.

Carlos loved his work and loved being part of Badlands life, but he could sense things changing. Recently, President Peregrine took over, and promised to modernize the country with exciting new technology. People loved him for it, but Carlos was old and wise and could see right through it. This pint-sized President had evil intentions, he knew that much.

Carl sat back and ran his hands down his face. He would change the names later, of course, and it was all well and good saying Peregrine had evil intentions, but what were they? Did he want to blow up the moon? Turn everyone into werewolves? What?

He looked around the granny flat for inspiration. Maybe Peregrine could cover the world with flowery wallpaper? Or turn people into porcelain figurines?

Ah, it was hopeless. Carl desperately needed a change of scenery. Maybe that would provide the inspiration he needed.

Pete and Sandra, yet again in the garden, were surprised to see Carl approach.

"How come you're not at work?" asked Pete, checking his watch.

Carl explained the scheme to them and watched as their faces shifted from confused to worried, then back to confused.

Sandra patted Carl's arm with a garden-gloved hand. "Are you sure it's that, Carl? If you're off work with stress, it's OK. We won't judge you."

"No!" Carl protested. "I'm telling the truth. There's a website and everything!"

Pete leaned on his rake and looked at his brother with a smile that displayed more than a hint of concern. "You can talk to us about anything, you know that, don't you?"

"About what?" said Carl.

Sandra leaned forwards and lowered her voice. "Your stress."

"I AM NOT STRESSED!" Carl snapped, then stomped up the garden, tripped over a gnome and slammed into the fence.

Pete and Sandra looked at each other, the pity on their faces dialled up to ten. "Poor man," Sandra whispered.

Carl walked along the canal, thinking the story through, but his every turn led to nothing. This is what had stopped him last time: writer's block. But how to get around it now? He stood on the hill which overlooked Fishwick and the surrounding areas, the fields spread out into the distance like a patchwork quilt. Somewhere in the tight grey grids of the town was his old house. He wondered what Kate was doing, and Indie, and Alex.

He worried about Alex the most. He was such a sensitive boy. How was he going to handle all of this? He needed his dad.

Chapter Ten

I'm bending over to pick up a parcel that Lloyd and Miriam had tipped on to the grimy rug when a samurai runs up behind me and stabs me in the back with his sword. At least that's what it feels like.

"Aaaauuurgghhhhhh!"

"Everything all right over there?" I hear Miriam ask.

I mean, obviously it's not, Miriam. I'm bent double in screaming agony.

"It's my back," I wheeze.

I hear Lloyd chuckle. "Young people of today. No stamina. Right, let's get you sorted."

"What do you mean, 'get me sorted'?" I manage to hiss. Oh man, this hurts so much.

"I'm the designated first aider in this depot, so I

know what I'm doing," he says. "I decided to train after I lost the end of my finger in that bungee jumping accident."

"Didn't your certificate run out a year ago?" asks Miriam.

"Ehh, things can't have changed that much since then," said Lloyd. "Right, first of all, Alex, I'm going to have to straighten you up."

"No!" I yelp.

"So, what, you want to spend the rest of your life hunched over like Quasimodo?" he says. "Best to do it quick. It'll be like ripping off a plaster."

"I don't think that applies to spines!" I whimper, but it's too late. In one quick motion, Lloyd has straightened me up.

Oh. Actually, that doesn't feel so bad.

Wait – am I supposed to feel numb from the neck down?

"Right, now go and lie down on the floor over there," he says, pointing at the damp, drafty corner by the toilet.

I try to convince him that's not necessary, but he plays his first aider card and makes me do it. I notice the mousetrap by the wall, centimetres away. Ugh. The pain in my back is right between my shoulder blades and the pressure does kind of help.

Once all the packages are sorted, Lloyd tells me to get up. It's still a bit sore, but not as bad as it was.

"Carrying heavy bags, eh?" he chuckles.

I nod.

"That's why they don't normally have kids doing this job," says Miriam. "How about you take one of our trolleys?"

"I've already got one," I say.

Miriam laughs lightly. "Oh, you haven't seen nothing yet!"

She goes out to the van and comes back with a smaller trolley, the kind you'd normally use to transport a bag of golf clubs. "Take this with you, clip a couple of bags to it, and you don't have to worry about getting a bad back. We don't use ours that often, so knock yourself out."

I imagine trying to navigate the streets with that trolley: wheelie bins, dog walkers and cars in my way, but at least it's got to be better than paralysing myself.

It's another busy day, with nearly as much mail and parcels as yesterday. At least today the weather is nicer, so I tuck Brenda's raincoat in the storage space under the trolley.

The lightweight trolley, which I tuck inside the big one, makes clearing the bags easier and today I don't feel like my lungs are going to burst out my chest when I reach the top of Sunset Hill.

My phone buzzes in my pocket as I begin the third bag. Message from Dad. I texted him first thing, asking how the book was coming along, but he hadn't replied. Now he's sent me three thumbs-up emojis.

I smile as I put my phone back and start pushing the freshly loaded trolley. It's working! My plan is on track! I give Christmas Mick a friendly wave as I pass by. He's out front, changing his "days to Christmas" sign from one to zero.

The sun comes peeking out from behind the clouds. Today is going to be a better day than yesterday. I just know it.

Chapter Eleven

A black blur flies out of a dark passageway around the side of the house. I spin around to face it, but before I can make sense of it, I'm knocked to the floor, pinned down.

Hot meat-smelling air blasts my face and I'm covered in strings of slobber. Oh my God, it's a dog. Was there even a sticker on this address? Did I check?

I try and scramble away, but the dog is on me, snapping in my face. My arms are jammed by my sides, but I manage to tap my pocket. My phone is present, but even if I slip it out, how am I going to dial anyone without being mauled to death?

I kick out, but all that does is make the dog angrier and its foaming jaws grow ever closer to my face. I rack my brain for any information about what to do in the event of an animal attack. Should I play dead? Should I try and make myself big? Should I poo my pants?

"HEEEEELP!" I scream. "HEEEEEEELP!"

I have nothing to fight off the beast with. Not even my scanner, which is nestled in one of my bags on the little trolley.

"Oh my word! Babs, get off him this instant!"

The dog jumps off me and sits obediently, still staring at me. The owner, a man in a cardigan and *Star Wars* slippers, comes running out of the house.

"Are you OK?" he asks.

I stand up and dust myself down. "Well, the dog didn't kill me," I say.

"Oh, Babs wouldn't hurt a fly," the man says. "She's just protective, that's all. Are you delivering papers or something?"

"P-post," I stammer, passing him the now dog-spit-soaked brown envelope.

"Ah," says the man. "She's fine with our usual chap. He just brings her a little biscuit."

Mental note: get biscuits.

"Yeah, you love Carl, don't you, girl?" the man

says, ruffling the coarse fur on top of Babs's head. "Everyone loves Carl around here."

Yeah, I'm starting to get that impression. I wonder if Dad really knows it, though?

The Reunion

Carlos knew someone had to stop President Peregrine's evil plan (WHAT IS IT????? THINK, CARL, THINK!) but he couldn't find the energy. When he was a younger man, he would have made a better go of it, but now he was an empty shell. He lived alone in a remote shack in the middle of the desert, miles away from his family home, where he had spent many happy years with his wife and two children.

Carlos could pinpoint the exact moment things went wrong. It was when he went to a school reunion in Harvey City. He hadn't seen his old pal Stan since they were teenagers. They had some great times back then, the two stars in the soccer team. He was hanging out with Stan when he first met Kate and his life changed for ever. Then Stan went off to university and that was that.

Now Stan stood before Carlos a fully grown man, with only a hint of the boy he remembered in the lines of his face.

"What are you doing these days, Carlos?" he boomed, slapping him on the shoulder.

"I work for the postal service in the Badlands," said Carlos. "How about you?"

Stan grinned wide and pulled a business card out of his pocket, pressing it into Carlos's hand. Carlos looked down at the crisp white rectangle. JoyCorp. Carlos knew JoyCorp. Everybody did. They made everything from cars to toothpaste. That company had to be worth millions, if not billions. Stan must be doing pretty well working for them.

"That's my company, Carlos," said Stan. "Built it up myself and now I got my own villa in the Caribbean."

Carlos felt sick. JoyCorp was *his* company? How had his old friend reached such heights, while he was delivering letters in the desert? And even that was about to come to an end.

After that, Carlos was never the same.

Carl read back what he'd written. Those same emotions that boiled up after the real school reunion began to swirl in his stomach and he knew that would make the writing better, but did he really want to go through all that again? To be reminded what a failure he was?

Carl slammed the laptop lid down and turned on the TV. That was enough writing for the day.

Chapter Twelve

Ah, Saturday. What a week it's been. I've run into a fountain, got soaking wet three times, got sunburnt once and was nearly murdered by a bloodthirsty dog called Babs.

But it's not all been bad. Lloyd and Miriam are really helpful, and everyone I've met has been nice. Even Babs is friendly now I've brought a little pack of biscuits with me.

Another thing is I'm always having to answer the same questions:

"Where's Carl?"

"When will he be back?"

There are also the slightly annoying:

"Oh, but Carl is normally here earlier."

"Carl knows to leave our parcels in the greenhouse."

It's like Dad knows literally everyone in the village and everyone misses him.

"Wotcha, we've got a leaker!" Lloyd holds up a box with a huge jet of water shooting out of the bottom corner.

"Crikey!" says Miriam. "What have they ordered? A pre-filled watering can?"

Lloyd squints at the box. "Caution. Live fish inside." He chuckles. "Not for much longer."

"Hold on," I say. "We can't let them die!"

"Well, what do you suggest?" says Lloyd. "Drop it in the toilet?"

I run into the bathroom, jam the grimy plug into the sink and run the cold tap as fast as it will go. Then I sprint back, grab the box from Lloyd, rip off the tape and find the fish inside, gasping in a clear bag. I put it into the sink as the water rises, freeing it from the plastic.

"Come on, you silly tap," I growl, as it sluggishly fills the bowl.

The fish is like a goldfish, but bigger. Its long body is mostly white with occasional orange-red blushes. I gently push its face towards the deeper water in the centre of the basin.

Since when can you send live fish through the

post, anyway? Surely that has to be against the law?

With the water level at the maximum, the fish begins to stir and soon it is swimming around quite happily. Miriam and Lloyd come in to see it.

"Never mind being a postman, you could have been a vet," says Lloyd, digging me in the ribs. "I haven't seen such quick action for a fish since that piranha attacked my hand in the Amazon back in '72."

I turn and examine the box to see where it's bound. My heart sinks to the depths.

"What the blazes is going on?" Mr Greenwood booms at me from his front doorstep.

His face is as pink as the flowers that line his garden path. I couldn't believe it. Of all the people on my round, why did it have to be him? The serial complainer? The grumpiest man in the western hemisphere?

"I'm sorry, sir," I say. "The box sprung a leak, but I saved the fish's life." I hold up the dirty plastic bucket Lloyd found around the back of the depot.

Mr Greenwood looks at it like it's a microwave dish full of mouldy beef.

"That's typical of your company, isn't it?" he says. "You treat our precious parcels like you're airport baggage handlers. Shoddy! Well, your boss will be hearing about this!"

My heart drops. If he complains to Peregrine, I'm finished.

"I'm sorry, Mr Greenwood!" I blurt. "But if it weren't for me, the fish would be dead! Please don't complain to my boss!"

Greenwood seems to consider this for a second, his deeply wrinkled scowl temporarily softening, but then he shakes his head fast and glares at me again. "Well, what I want to know is why do they have children delivering for them?"

"I'm just helping out!" I protest.

He leans back into his house and picks up the pizza and funeral leaflets, scrunching them in his hand. "Well, if you're helping, then maybe you can tell me how many times I'm going to have to tell you people I don't want these rrrrrruddy leaflets!"

I can see why Dad doesn't like this guy. He has the nastiest eyes I've ever seen, magnified by glasses that take up half his face.

"Sorry," I mumble again.

"Sorry's not going to cut it this time," he moans.

"It should be on record that I don't want this junk." His face is going so red he looks like he's going to explode. Maybe the funeral leaflet will come in handy after all.

I don't want to look at his horrible face, so I stare at the fish instead, who seems to be looking back at me as if to say, "You've brought me to live with him? Why didn't you just let me die?"

"Anyway," Greenwood goes on, "what's happened to the old one? Did they actually listen to my complaint and sack him?"

My eyes snap back up to his face. "You asked them to sack him?"

Greenwood smirks. "Of course I did. Unprofessional conduct, calling me names, thinking I can't hear him."

"Have you ever considered that he called you names because you're a horrible person?" My mouth blurts it out before my brain can tell me it's a bad idea.

"I BEG YOUR PARDON?"

"Well, I don't think he calls anyone else names. In fact, I know he doesn't. It's probably because you spoke to him like dirt, because you have a phobia of leaflets."

Greenwood starts going a darker shade of purple and I begin to back away.

"I have never known such impertinence!"

"And I've never known anyone who doesn't just throw leaflets in the bin rather than shout at people who are just doing their jobs!" I say, my silly mouth running again.

This time, I carefully place the bucket down and retreat all the way back down the path, the old goblin grumbling at me as I go.

That might have been a mistake.

Carl slapped the side of the ancient TV as if that would make football appear on it. No good. In his other hand was his phone, pressed against his ear. The company had him on hold for half an hour and he was sick of hearing the same dreary classical music piece over and over again. They could at least liven it up and play something good to keep you entertained.

"Hello, you're through to Cloud TV customer services. My name is Kevin. How may I help you?"

Carl was so shocked that someone actually answered, he almost dropped the phone.

"Yes, hello. I paid for the sports package last night and it's not coming on my TV."

Carl had been trying all morning and nothing he did could make it happen. Why did everything have to be so complicated? He was having a break from the book for a while. Just a while. He told himself that watching football would re-energize him. Maybe even inspire him. After all, football matches are stories. Kind of? Maybe?

"Ah. I'm sorry to hear that, sir. First thing I need to do is check if you've updated your Cloud TV app."

Carl scratched his head. "App? What app?"

"Yes, sir, you need to download the app in order to activate the sports package. I can send the QR code if it will help."

Carl closed his eyes and took a deep breath. He used to think he was pretty with it when it came to technology. When he brought that iPod into work years ago, not long after they came out, Miriam and Lloyd acted like it was something off *Star Trek*. But then he seemed to look away for five minutes and the whole world changed. Apps? QR codes? What happened to paying for a thing and just having it? What happened to delivering letters and parcels without everything having to be tracked and snooped on by apps?

But Carl wasn't too downhearted. This conversation was inspiring him already and he could feel the laptop pulling him back over…

Chapter Thirteen

Dinner last night was the same as every night. Mum and Indie teased me about my fake bike ride and my mystery girlfriend, while I struggled not to fall asleep. Ah well, at least I'm on to week two now. That's almost halfway there.

I'm starting to get a bit more used to the job now. I don't have to think about what to press on the scanner any more; my fingers just sort of do it by themselves.

So far this morning, Christmas Mick has given me a cracker, I saw Brenda by the shops and she asked me why I wasn't wearing the raincoat she's given me even though it's roasting and I managed to avoid old Greenwood. I don't have much more to do now. It helps that it's been a quieter day: a lot fewer letters and not as many parcels.

Near the canal bridge, there is a row of three houses set back from the main road. I have post for the middle one and am about to shove it through when the door opens. (This has happened before, and it always terrifies people. Once an old lady opened the door while looking to her side and when she turned to see me standing there, letters in hand, she screamed and had to sit down. I tried not to be offended.) This time, again, the man who opened the door isn't looking. He's talking to someone behind him.

"It's lovely," he's saying. "The bedrooms in particular: so much bigger than we were expecting."

"I'm glad you liked it," a voice from behind says. I recognize the voice instantly – and jump to the side before she has the chance to see me.

I won't have time to escape to the main road, so I'm going to have to hide.

I run down to the side of the house and crouch behind the bin. When I peer out, I see Mum's work car parked in the drive. On it, a huge sticker that says: *Barson's Estate Agency.*

Oh no. What are the odds I'd come to a house that Mum is showing someone round?

"We'll have a chat about it and get back to you," the man says.

"That's fine," says Mum. "There is a little bit of interest in the property so I wouldn't leave it too long, though."

I hear another woman's voice pipe up. "Sorry, could we just have one last look at the back garden before we go?"

I glance around. The gate is barely two metres away from me. *Say no, Mum. Tell her you haven't got time.*

"Yes, of course!"

NO, Mum!

They come around the side of the house while I curl myself into the tiniest ball I can, letters still in hand. I'm not a person, I'm just some rubbish. Pay no attention. Pay no attention.

From my cricked-neck position, I can see Mum fiddling with the handle to get the gate open.

"It's a little stiff," the man says.

"Nothing a bit of WD40 won't fix," says Mum, still yanking at the handle.

While this is happening, the woman is turning around and she's … she's looking right at me. Desperately, I shake my head as much as I can and put my finger to my lips. She stares at me, frowning like she's trying to figure out whether to say anything.

CLUNK!

"Hey, we're in!" says Mum.

The woman stares at me for another couple of seconds, then follows them into the garden. That's it, I'm out of here. As soon as the gate clangs shut again, I run down the drive and back to the main road. I need to get back to my lightweight trolley because there are a few letters still in there and I left it unattended a little longer than I would normally, what with having to hide by a bin and everything.

Wait a second. Where is it? I could have sworn I left it under this tree.

It's gone. It's actually gone. I wasn't even away that long! Who knew Fishwick was such a crime-infested hellhole? My mind flits straight to calling the police, because that's what you do when something is stolen, but what could I say? I'm pretty sure what I'm doing is illegal, isn't it?

Whoever took it can't have gone far. I look down the slope of the road as it winds down towards the centre of the village. No sign of it. I turn and look up the hill, using my hand to shield my eyes from the sun. I see two figures standing on the canal bridge, looking down at me.

I squint hard, hoping it isn't them. Praying it isn't them.

But it is.

"What have you done with my trolley?" I yell as I run towards them.

Holden and Greg snigger, nudging each other. I knew it would be only a matter of time before they tried something again, but I was hoping for a little bit longer.

"We haven't got it," says Holden.

I look all around, checking behind them as they lean on the wall of the bridge.

"Where is it?" I say, trying to catch my breath.

"We're doing a science experiment," says Greg.

"What are you talking about?" I ask, my voice flat.

"We wanted to see if it would float," says Greg.

Hot daggers of panic slice into my brain. *No. They haven't.* I lean over the side and see the trolley half submerged in the brown water of the canal, bags and all.

"*I* said it would sink, but Greg said it would

float," says Holden. "Looks like I'm going to be right in the end."

I can see water spilling over the sides of the bags. I growl and without a second thought, shove Greg against the wall.

Holden steps in and pushes me back with one hand. "You better get your little trolley, yeah?"

Greg sniggers. "Not so hard now you don't have your little old lady to protect you, are you?"

I push past them and scramble down the slope on to the towpath. The trolley is right in the middle of the canal. There's no way I'll be able to reach it.

"Get your water wings on then, Ally!" Holden hoots from the bridge.

I am going to get those two. I don't know how, but I will.

There's a pretty big tree branch lying at the foot of a hedge. I snatch it up and reach across the water, but it gets nowhere near the trolley. Holden and Greg keep jeering at me from the bridge, but I try to tune them out.

I glimpse over the edge, past the long grass choked with stingers, down into the water. It's so dark, it could be up to my knees or over my head. And who knows what could be down there?

I try reaching over with the branch again, pushing my reach to the limit, but it's no use.

Holden and Greg must have got bored of laughing at me because they're gone now. Maybe I could go home, put on some wellies and come back? But the trolley will have sunk by then. Oh, this is a nightmare. The trolley is lost.

"Hey."

A quiet voice cuts through the silence. I turn to my left and see a girl looking at me. My heart does this weird flip when I recognize her from the barge, the black cat curling itself around her legs. She's holding a long piece of rope with what looks like a black bell dangling off it. Her eyes are narrowed and her mouth is in a serious line.

"Hello," I say.

"Want me to get your trolley back?" she asks.

I nod. "Um, yes, please."

"Name's Willow." Although it's quiet, her voice is tough, like leather.

"Alex," I say.

She bends and touches the cat on its head. It gently purrs, then slowly saunters to the hedge, where it lies down and stretches in the sun.

Willow stands on the edge of the path, the toes

of her trainers hanging over. The sole of her left one is beginning to come away.

She bunches up the rope, then casts it out into the canal. The bell hits the leg of the trolley with a loud clunk, and it seems to attach itself. Then she begins to pull the rope, dragging the trolley towards her. Her face twists into a grimace as she pulls. I feebly ask if she needs any help, but she ignores and keeps yanking until the trolley is by the bank. I go over and help her drag it out on to the path.

"Wow," I say. "Thanks."

Willow prises the bell off the trolley and coils the rope back up. "Magnet fishing can be pretty useful sometimes."

I frown. "Magnet fishing? What's that?"

"What it sounds like." She sniffs. "You throw it in the canal and pull out metal stuff. Sometimes you find things you can sell for scrap." She peers into my bags. "They look soggy. You should dry them off on my boat."

The way she says it makes it seem like it's not a question, and now she's grabbed my trolley and is wheeling it up the towpath. I follow, with the cat just behind. As I walk, I bend to try and stroke her, but she dodges me and trots ahead until she's level with Willow. When we reach the boat, the cat hops up on to the roof and lies on her back, rolling from side to side.

Willow stops the trolley on the path, unbuckles the bags and throws them on to the little area with the stick people use to steer boats. I've never been on a barge before so I don't know the names of any of the parts. She reaches in, pulls out the remaining few letters and lies them on the roof by the cat.

"Pass me some stones, will you?" she says. "Pretty big ones."

The towpath is rough and embedded with stones of all sizes, so I prise out the biggest ones I can find. Willow takes them from me with a nod, then uses them to weigh down the letters. She hangs the bags on the steering stick.

"They should dry out pretty quick," she says, folding her arms. "You want to come in and wait?"

It doesn't look like I have much choice. It's either that or stand outside awkwardly. I check my pockets. Phone? *Present.* Wallet? *Present.* Willow opens the little door and heads inside the boat. I take a look around, then follow.

Inside, it smells of damp and cat. There is a small

table and chair stood opposite a cooker, with a mini fridge set into a counter. At the far end, there are two single beds. The wooden floor is almost completely covered by a thin rug – a little like the one at the depot.

Willow fills a metal kettle at the tap, then pulls a match from a yellow box, lights up a hob and sets the kettle on the flame. I've never seen anything like it outside of a museum.

"You want tea?" she asks, but she's already pulling down two mugs and throwing a tea bag into a pot.

"OK," I say. I only ever drink tea at my nan's house, and that's just because she never has Dr Pepper in her cupboards.

"So are you on holiday?" I ask.

Willow tucks a tightly coiled strand of red hair behind her ear. "No. This is where I live."

I scan her face for any sign that she's joking. I mean, I couldn't imagine living on one of these things. For a second, the horrifying thought of being permanently stuck in such a cramped space with Indie and Mum flashes through my mind. Willow looks on, stone-faced. She's not joking.

"Oh," I say. "That's … interesting?"

Willow's pale blue eyes flash into an expression I can't quite figure out. "Right. Well, me and Mum prefer it this way. Why don't you sit down?" She nods at the table. I take a seat in a creaky orange plastic chair.

"So it's just you and your mum, then?"

Willow nods. "That's right. I'm guessing you live in a mansion with both your parents, eight siblings and a litter of puppies?"

I giggle nervously as the kettle begins to whistle like a ghostly train in the night. "No, normal house. And it's just me, my mum and my sister. Dad moved out."

Willow raises an eyebrow and pulls a small carton of milk from the fridge. "That why you've got a job? Helping to pay the bills?"

What am I supposed to tell her? Well, no, actually, it's because I want my dad to write a book so he can be happy again and so Mum will take him back? I'd sound like I'd just smacked my head on something.

"Yeah," I say. "Got to do my bit."

Willow picks up the kettle with one hand and turns off the hob with the other. She moves smoothly, like she's done this thousands of times.

"So where is your mum now?" I ask.

Willow carefully fills the teapot with boiling water. "She's got a little job around here," she replies. "Just for the summer."

"Oh," I say. "So are you not from around here?"

Willow shakes her head. "That's the thing about living on a barge: home can be anywhere. But we're normally moored in a marina in another town."

"Which town?" I ask.

Willow turns her back on me, removes the lid of the teapot and stirs it with a stained spoon.

"Why did those kids throw your trolley in the cut?" she asks.

She'd definitely heard me ask what town she was from. Maybe she doesn't want to answer.

"They're just jerks," I say. "You must have jerks at your school."

Willow pours tea into the mugs and tops them off with a little milk. "Yep. I get called all kinds of names because of where I live."

Oh, man. I can imagine.

Willow brings the mugs over to the table and takes the chair opposite.

"Do you have any sugar?" I ask. I normally have

two. Sometimes two and a half if I feel like I need the energy.

Willow shakes her head. The cat must have slipped in at some point, because she's now sitting in Willow's lap, pawing at her trousers. Willow smiles; it's the first time I've seen her do it. One of her front teeth is a little chipped, and for some reason that makes my heart skip again. Weird. "Hello, little Madge," she coos.

Madge! *That's* the cat's name. I remember her saying it when I nearly ran her over that day.

"So how long have you been doing your job?" she asks me.

"A week," I say. I look around. There's no sign of a TV or games console. There are books, though. Loads of them, stacked on every surface. Every particle in my body wants to tidy them, to find a shelf and put them into alphabetical order like the ones in my room, but I can't. *It's not your boat, Alex. Her boat, her rules, her lack of any obvious sorting system.*

Willow runs a hand along Madge's back. Her purr is a deep, low rumble. "You haven't come across an Eve Haunton, have you?"

I think about it. I don't remember many names

because I just look at addresses, and the only ones that have stuck out are Christmas Mick, Brenda and that moaning old man Greenwood's – oh, and that one man on High Street called Willy Payne. I laugh every time I see that one.

"No, sorry," I say. "Why? Is that someone you know?"

Willow picks up her mug and blows off some steam. "I can help you, if you want?"

"With my job?" I say, trying to keep up with Willow's random changes to the conversation.

Willow nods. "We could split the work between us and share thc money."

Ah. Now, this could be a problem. See, I like the idea of splitting the work in half, but I'm not getting any money.

"The thing is," I say, my mouth blurting out the truth before my brain can come up with something better, "I'm not actually getting paid."

Willow carefully places her mug back down. "But you said you were helping to pay the bills."

I blink hard. "Yeah. Sorry. This is actually more of a work experience type thing."

Willow chuckles. "Getting your stuff thrown off a bridge? What an experience."

I laugh a little too. I have to laugh or I will cry.

"OK, well how about this?" says Willow. "I'll help you do your job and instead of money, you could sort me out with some food."

"Food? Are you hungry or something?"

Willow takes a deep breath. "We don't have much money. That means we struggle with shopping."

I can't imagine what that must be like. No matter what has happened in our house, there's always been food.

"OK," I say. "I'm sure I can get you something."

Willow smiles. "You got a deal, Alex. I'll start tomorrow, yeah?"

I nod. "Sounds good."

The Microchip

Carlos had been a postman in the Badlands most of his life. He didn't let anything stop him doing his job. He battled through sandstorms, dodged tornados and kept himself alive after his truck broke down, by drinking from his radiator. One time he even sucked venom out of his own arm after a rattler struck.

This time, though, it was different. The threat wasn't coming from the Badlands, it was coming from outside, thundering over the horizon like a twister, and the poison couldn't be sucked out this time.

The government wanted to use the residents of the Badlands as guinea pigs, giving all of them a microchip implant in their brains. Messages would now be received instantaneously, meaning there would be no need for letters and Carlos's livelihood was about to be destroyed.

He pulled his bike over outside Christmas Mick's white fence, enveloped in red and green bulbs. The daylight was clear, bright and burning almost every day in the desert, so there was no need for the lights to be turned on, yet they always were. Until now.

Carlos's stomach twisted. Something must have gone wrong if Christmas Mick had switched his lights off. As he walked up the path, the animatronic elf, which always sang "Jingle Bells" when anyone moved anywhere near it, was silent, its faded eyes staring into infinity, partially melted by the sun.

Carlos rapped the flaking wooden door. "Mickey," he called out. "You there?"

He pressed the doorbell, which normally played "Silent Night", but nothing happened. He knocked again and the door opened. Mick smiled at Carlos, but there was something about his face that turned Carlos's stomach. Mick's eyes were as cold and dead as a shark. Instead of his usual Christmas tree top, he wore a sensible shirt and tie.

"Hello, Carlos, so wonderful to see you," he said in a flat voice.

"Mickey," said Carlos, slightly backing away. "What happened to you?"

Mick, still blankly grinning, bent his head forward and showed Carlos a small shaved patch.

"They put my microchip in, Carlos," he said. "It's wonderful."

Carlos stepped back again. It was like someone had replaced Mick with a badly designed robot.

"Oh yeah?" he said, filled with horror.

"Yeeeeeesssss," Mick droned. "Thank you, President Peregrine. All hail your glorious regime."

Carlos beat it back to his truck and slammed the door. Mick was still standing on his porch, smiling that shark smile.

Carlos had to put a stop to this. He couldn't let the Badlands fall. Because if that happened, the rest of the country – no, the rest of the world! – would follow.

Carl sat back and read his work so far. It was better. At least he'd figured out Peregrine's evil scheme. It was pretty clever, the more he thought about it. These microchips represented all the technology that was taking over the real world. Emails instead of letters, apps instead of, well, everything.

The problem was, he had no idea what to write next. How was a postman going to fight back against the government? He was just one man! Where would he even start?

He needed some help. On his other attempts at writing books, he always talked to Kate about them, but that wasn't an option now. Or was it? Maybe he could talk to her about this one, show her he was making an effort? He left the granny flat, then went back inside, then went back outside, then back in.

*

"What are you looking at, love?" asked Pete, coming into the kitchen for a drink.

Sandra stood by the sink, looking out of the window towards the granny flat. "He keeps walking in and out of the house, Pete. I think he might be having a breakdown."

Chapter Fourteen

"You know, the strangest thing happened today," says Mum, taking a sip of water after finishing dinner. "I was showing a couple around a house, and the woman said she saw a boy hiding by the bins."

My eyes shoot open. I am so tired I was dropping off.

"Oh really?" I say, staring intently at my corn on the cob.

"Yes," says Mum. "And when I went back to have a look, there was no sign of any boy."

"That's really weird," I say. "She didn't describe him, did she?"

"Not really," Mum replies. "Just that he looked pale and scary."

Wow. Thanks, lady.

"So what was up with her?" says Indie, looking up from her phone. "Was she hallucinating, or what?"

"Well, I just assumed it was kids messing about, but this woman was convinced she'd seen a ghost," says Mum, rolling her eyes.

Indie splutters with laughter. "Jeez."

"They were really keen on the house too," says Mum. "Now she's refusing to even consider putting in an offer because she reckons the house is haunted." She sighs and rubs her forehead. "I've heard it all now."

Great. So while doing Dad's job, I've somehow managed to ruin Mum's. Nice going, Alex.

The front door clicks open.

"Only me!"

Me, Indie and Mum look at each other. Mum's jaw clenches and she turns around in her chair to face the door to see Dad walking in.

"Evening, family!"

"Carl, how many times? You can't just show up unannounced like this."

Dad's smile shrivels. It's like he's been punctured. "But it's my house too."

Mum turns back and faces us. "I'm not doing this again."

Dad comes over and takes his seat at the table. The one he always had. Now the table is complete. The Natural Order of Things. I give him a smile. So does Indie, I notice.

"Look, I'm not going to stay long," he says. "I just thought you might like to know that I've started writing again."

Mum clasps her hands together, her elbows resting on the table. "I'm happy for you, I really am. But that doesn't change things. I need you to call ahead in future."

My stomach feels like it's been kicked.

"Fine," says Dad. "I'll call ahead. I've got plenty of spare time this summer anyway."

The kicked feeling in my stomach begins to change into something far more panicky.

"Oh, why's that?" says Mum.

Dad leans over and ruffles my hair. "It's all thanks to this little rascal. He found out about a work scheme where I can have paid time off to write!"

I sense Mum and Indie both staring at me even though I'm not looking at them.

"Wow," says Mum. "Very clever. And very generous of your employer. Why didn't you sort me out with something like that, Alex?"

I continue to stare at my half-empty glass as if I could create a distraction by hurling it at the wall with my mind.

"Sorry," I mumble.

"Oh, hey," says Indie. "I just need a word with you in private, Alex."

I look over at Dad. He's holding a stack of paper. Is that the book? Then I remember Indie's question.

"What's it about?" I ask Indie.

"Oh, just school stuff," she says, breezily. "Come on."

"But Dad—"

Indie gets up and pinches the back of my neck. "Mum and Dad need some time alone, I think. Come on."

I reluctantly follow Indie upstairs. For a second, I think I'm actually going to be allowed into her room for the first time in about five years, but instead she steers me into the spare room and closes the door behind us. Before I can speak, she's jabbing me in the chest.

"You are going to spill it," she says. "Now."

"I don't know what you're talking about," I say.

Indie folds her arms. "You are a terrible liar, Alexander. Now, I know you're up to something. Sneaking around in here, disappearing every day, and now I'm hearing about some scheme? What company in their right mind is going to pay someone to stay at home and write a book? It's ridiculous!"

"It's true," I say, nodding probably a bit too hard. "There's a website and everything! And I've told you: I'm just going out on bike rides."

"Whatever it is you're trying, you need to stop," says Indie. "You can't interfere with Mum and Dad's lives. You've got to let it go." She takes a deep breath. "I have a mantra, if it will help."

"A 'mantra'? Isn't that a snake?" I ask.

Indie flicks my forehead. "No, silly. A mantra, an affirmation." She closes her eyes. "I am but a twig on the shoulders of a mighty stream."

"What's that supposed to mean?" I ask.

"It's acceptance," says Indie, talking to me like my one remaining brain cell has just popped. "Letting go of the idea that you are in control."

I don't want to hear this. I *am* in control. This is all under my power. I can do this.

Mum and Dad are talking downstairs. I can't hear the words, but the tone doesn't sound friendly.

"Look, I'm not interfering," I say to Indie.

Indie narrows her eyes at me. "Just cut it out," she says. "Or else."

Chapter Fifteen

When I turn on my lights this morning, I see a small piece of card shoved under my door. On it are some typewritten words, so I know it's from Indie.

I am but a twig on the shoulders of a mighty stream.

Yeah, thanks for that. I drop it in my bin on the way out.

It's Willow's first day helping me out. The easiest thing would be to message Willow when I'm out of the depot, but the problem is she doesn't have a phone. I can't believe someone my age doesn't have a phone. I know she said they didn't have much money, but *everyone* has a phone. Even me, and I barely have anyone to talk to. Well, besides Spencer, but I've been ignoring his constant bragging messages from France. So annoying.

I push my trolley to the top of the hill for my first bag. It's not too bad today: light on letters and not that many parcels. Ideal for a first day.

Willow arrives at exactly nine fifteen, just as we arranged. She's wearing sunglasses that look too big for her face and her hair is piled into a tatty baseball cap.

"Well," I say. "You look different."

"When you're a redhead like me, you've got to take care in the sun," she says. "So anyway, what do you want me to do?"

I pull out a small bag with just letters in it. "All you have to do is post these," I say. "And while you're doing that, I'll do parcels." I hold up my scanner.

"Sounds all right," Willow says, with a nod. "Anything I should know?"

"For now, just that there's a man over the road who acts like it's permanently Christmas," I say. "Later on, there'll be grumpy old men and vicious dogs, but we'll worry about them when we get there."

Willow takes the bag, slings it over her shoulder and heads down the hill.

*

It only feels like five minutes later when we finish.

"How about that?" says Willow, with a chipped-tooth grin. "Teamwork makes the dream work."

We carry on like that with every bag, getting through it super quick every time. When we're halfway through, we take a break. I use my pocket money to buy us a chocolate bar, a bag of crisps and a drink each, and we sit on a bench opposite the shop, the trolley chained to a street sign nearby.

"So what do you think of it so far?" I ask.

"Easy," Willow chomps through a mouthful of crisps. She has cheese and onion while I have ready salted. "Just pushing paper through holes. I have no idea how you don't bore yourself to death."

I shrug. "I've got plenty of things to think about."

Willow seems to consider this for a second, then drops one of her crisps into my crisps bag, motioning for me to return the favour. "Makes it a bit more exciting. How long until we get to the mystery crisp?"

I laugh a little, even if the idea of mixing crisps unnerves me. When I first met Willow, I thought she was just weird, but I'm starting to realize it's just her sense of humour. Her jokes are so subtle, delivered with a completely straight face, that it's sometimes hard to tell she's not serious.

"So how come you're spending your summer doing this?" she asks. "Wouldn't you rather be hanging out with your friends?"

"I've only really got one friend, to be honest," I say. "And he's in France all summer."

"Ooh la la," says Willow, waggling her eyebrows. "So you just thought, hey, I'll be a postman for no money? Oh, mystery crisp!"

With my own bag already finished, I open my chocolate bar to give my hands something to do. "Yeah, pretty much. It will look good on my, um, college application?"

Willow looks at me with that same narrow-eyed expression she fixed me with last night. I can sense she doesn't buy it. I could tell her, admit to the whole scam. But I don't know her that well. How do I know I can trust her?

"Hey," I say. "Who was that person you asked me about the other day? Eve something, wasn't it?"

Willow tips the crumbs from her crisp packet into her mouth, then begins folding it up into a triangle. Dad always does that too. "Eve Haunton. She's just a family friend. I know she moved somewhere around here. Mum was asking about her, that's all."

She isn't looking at me while she speaks. Instead, she's staring off into the distance, at a figure walking towards us from the top of the street.

The person approaching us is beginning to look familiar. I'm hoping it's not him, but the closer he gets, the fainter my hope; it's obvious from his angry stride and pink face.

"Oh, I was hoping to run into you," Mr Greenwood barks, standing in front of us with an empty shopping bag folded under his arm. Willow gives me a "who is this guy" look, but I can't answer.

"Hello, Mr Greenwood," I say.

"Don't you hello Mr Greenwood me!" he snaps.

I'm not sure what I'm supposed to say now, so I keep quiet.

"After you were so impertinent last week, I called your boss to complain," he says.

That's not good. I try and keep a lid on my terror and clench my jaw. "OK," I say. Wallet: *present*. Phone: *present*.

"OK *indeed*." Greenwood smirks. "Well, when I told him he had a child working for him, a leaflet-instruction-ignoring child, a fish-mishandling child, he said he didn't know what I was talking about. He said the regulations were quite clear: no under-eighteens, et cetera, et cetera. He tried to fob me off, saying you must work for a different delivery company, but I know the truth. So come on. Out with it. What are you up to?"

Willow snorts. "You need to relax, mate."

Greenwood's gaze fixes on Willow for the first time. "If I wanted your opinion I'd ask for it, young…" He stops suddenly and leans forward, squinting through his thick glasses. "Hang about, do you have ginger hair under that hat?"

"None of your business," she fires back.

"Tell me!"

"Oh my God, you're such a weirdo," she says. "I'm a kid. You can't go around asking to look under kids' hats."

Mr Greenwood straightens up, his face going even pinker. "You look like the girl I saw stealing fruit from my garden last week! I caught you on my CCTV."

Willow folds her arms. "I didn't steal anything from your scabby old garden."

Mr Greenwood acts like he's been slapped. He points a trembling finger at me, then at Willow.

"You two are trouble," he says, "and I'm going to put a stop to it."

Willow makes a sarcastic "I'm so scared" gesture as Greenwood stomps into the shop behind us.

When he's gone, she rolls her eyes at me. "What a miserable old goat."

I laugh, and look down at my chocolate bar. Suddenly I'm not hungry. Sure, Peregrine denied that any kids are working for him, but he's going to be suspicious now.

"You all right?" Willow punches my thigh. "He hasn't got to you, has he?"

"'Course he hasn't," I say, hoping my lie isn't too obvious. "You weren't really stealing stuff from his garden, were you?"

Willow laughs and punches me again. "That's hilarious, Alex. The old geezer's probably just seeing things."

Kate

Carlos didn't know how to stop Peregrine's plan to implant a microchip in every Badlands resident's brain. Not the first clue. He sat in his lonesome shack that night and stared at the bare wooden walls, but came up with nothing. He would have to do what he always did when he needed inspiration: talk to Kate.

He cranked his Harley and sped out of the Badlands, watching as the landscape gradually transformed from rusty oranges and browns to lush greens. His old house sat atop a hill in the middle of a bustling town. Seeing so many people around was strange to Carlos, who had grown accustomed to living isolated out in the Badlands since Kate had kicked him out.

Carlos found the door to his former house open and walked inside. It didn't occur to him that he couldn't just do that. It still felt like his house, but when he saw Kate's face, the feeling faded.

"What are you doing here, Carlos?" she asked.

Carlos went to move towards her, but she stepped back. "Answer my question."

Carlos took a deep breath. "Where are Alex and Indie?"

"They're out," said Kate, flatly. "Now tell me why you're here."

Carlos didn't know how to begin. If he

said it out loud, he would sound delusional. *President Peregrine is implanting microchips in everyone's heads and I want to stop him.* Ridiculous.

Besides, Kate's *coldness* had taken the wind out of his sails. He knew he had caused this by slipping into his bad moods after the reunion, but her resentment ran deeper than that and he was only now beginning to realize it.

"Knock knock!"

Carl was so startled by Sandra walking into the granny flat that he accidentally flipped the laptop off the coffee table. She walked into the lounge, but she wasn't alone.

"Sorry to disturb you, Carl, but I've brought you a visitor."

The man walked out from behind Sandra. He was dressed all in black, with a white collar. He smiled at Carl, his eyes twinkling.

"This is Reverend Harris," said Sandra.

"I can see that!" said Carl, his face flushed. "But why have you brought him here? No offence, like."

Sandra smiled too. "I've been worried about you, Carl. Pete has too," she said. "You've been acting very strangely lately. And I just thought it would help to pray a little bit."

Carl groaned. "You're barking up the wrong tree, Sandra."

Sandra ignored Carl and rested a hand on his arm. "Please, just give it a go," she said.

Carl looked at the reverend and nodded. "All right. How about you ask the big man if he fancies writing another book? I hear the Bible was a pretty big seller."

Chapter Sixteen

I'm about to leave for work when I'm stopped by a monster.

"BAAAARRGH!"

Once I've had a second to get over the shock, I realize it's actually just Indie standing in front of the door. Her hair is all over the place and she has none of her usual make-up on.

"Off out on one of your bike rides, are you?" she says, hands on hips.

"Yep," I say, trying to push past her, but she takes a step to the side, blocking my way.

"I got up last night, Alex," she goes on. "And I had a hankering for a protein bar. Yet when I went to the cupboard, there were none there."

I shrug, trying to seem nonchalant, but probably

coming across very chalant indeed. “Maybe Mum had them?”

“You know as well as I do Mum hates them,” says Indie. “What’s going on? Are you trying to bulk up for your girlfriend?”

“No!” I snap.

“And not that it matters to me, but I noticed there’s a loaf of bread missing from the freezer too,” she says.

I grumble under my breath. When did Indie become a detective? It’s so annoying. Yeah, I’ve been taking bits of food every day and giving them to Willow, but I wasn’t expecting anyone to notice. I mean, we have loads of food.

“I’ve got to go,” I say.

“What’s in the bag?” asks Indie, nodding at the rucksack on my back.

Obviously, I know there is a half-frozen loaf in there, along with a big wodge of cheese wrapped in foil, but I’m not about to tell her that.

“None of your business, that’s what,” I say, and this time I’m able to wriggle past and get outside. As I hop on to my bike and push away, I can see her still watching me through the glass of the door.

*

“Happy Friday!” says Miriam as I walk into the depot.

“Not much happy about it,” grumbles Lloyd. “We’ve got to come in tomorrow, remember?”

I smile as I nudge my bag under Dad’s desk. I’m actually starting to like this job now I have Willow helping me. It’s been a few days now and we keep getting better and better. Greenwood has only had letters a couple of times and Willow gets around it by taking the side gate and ducking under the doorbell cam.

“Can’t prove anything without hard evidence, old man,” she says.

Besides that, everyone seems to like us. Brenda came out with ice lollies when it was hot on Wednesday and Christmas Mick gave Willow a little tinsel badge. Even Babs is warming to us.

And, of course, I’m always fielding questions about Dad. Willow doesn’t know the regular postman is my dad yet, but that hasn’t been a problem, especially as we mostly work separately.

We’re sorting parcels in the middle of the room. I’m starting to get quite good at it: I know *my* streets now; all the bird streets go to Lloyd and everything else is Miriam’s. Lloyd is loudly howling a guitar solo along with the radio when the phone rings.

It's still weird that they have a landline phone. It's cordless, but still; the only people I know who still have one are my grandparents.

Miriam grumbles as she steps over the pile and scoops up the phone. "If this is those kids prank calling again… Hello, Fishwick depot?"

I scoop up a parcel and fire it on to Miriam's desk without worrying about hitting her in the face. I'm sure if a health and safety person saw the way we work, they'd shut us down.

"But he's not here, Peregrine," says Miriam.

A tolling bell of doom bongs in my ribcage. Miriam is looking at me, confused. *Oh no. No, no, no.* She's going to find out my whole scheme. So is Peregrine. I need to do something. I hold out my hand for the phone. Miriam frowns at me. "Hang on a sec, Peregrine," she says, and hands it over.

I take the phone outside and close the door behind me. "What's going on?" Peregrine's voice honks down the line. It sounds like he's got a clothes peg on his nose.

This is not good. I need time to think of something.

"Um, hello," I say.

"To whom am I now speaking?"

To whom? Why does he talk like that? Is he a robot?

"This is Carl's … son," I say.

Oh, really nicely done, Alex. What a dynamite imagination you have.

"Riiiight. And may I ask why you're at the depot?"

"You may," I say.

The line goes quiet while my brain desperately scrambles for what I'm going to say next.

"OK," says Peregrine, beginning to sound even more peeved. "Why are you there?"

"Just stopping by on my way out," I say. "I won't be long."

I hear a faint sigh. "And where is your pops?"

"He's, uh, just gone to the shop," I say. "They needed tea bags."

That actually wasn't bad. I know they take it in turns to buy tea and milk. There's a rota and everything.

"OK, I'll call his mobile," says Peregrine.

"WAIT!" I yell. "WAIT, DON'T DO THAT."

The line goes quiet again.

"Are you still there?" I ask.

"Yes," Peregrine replies, crisply. "Now why shouldn't I call his mobile?"

"Becauuuuuuuse," I say, elongating the word while my brain scrambles for something … anything. "He dropped it down the toilet and it's not working. Can I take a message?"

"Fine," Peregrine huffs. "It's about this ongoing sitch with Mr Greenwood. He is persisting with his complaint and is now saying that kids are delivering mail. I don't suppose you know anything about that, do you, my man?"

I gulp and my dry throat clicks. "No," I say. "I mean, I did see some old guy and he accused me of delivering post, but I was just hanging around, I wasn't doing anything."

The line goes silent again. I remember seeing him do this to Dad a few weeks ago: just leaving a long gap so he'll fill it. I screw my eyes shut and lean against the wall. *Tough it out, Alex. Don't say anything that will get you into trouble.*

I start counting in my head. Anything to keep my brain busy. I get to twenty-five when Peregrine finally speaks.

"Hmm. Well, Mr Greenwood's claims did seem a bit out there. Because if it is true, it is highly illegal. I'm talking criminal charges territory."

The line goes quiet again. "OK," I finally say, with another gulp.

"Tell your old man I will keep an eye on the sitch and any further complaints will require a full investigation."

After he hangs up, I take a minute to gather myself.

I think I got away with it. Maybe.

I step back into the depot and place the phone back in its cradle. I'm hoping Miriam has forgotten about it.

"What was all that about?" she asks. "Why was Peregrine asking to speak to your dad?"

I force a chuckle, but it sounds like a choking goose. "He forgot he's off."

Lloyd laughs lightly. "So he is human after all."

I pick up a parcel from the rug, but Miriam is still looking at me, her eyebrows knitted. "He forgot?"

"Yeah," I say, still doing that pathetic chortle. "He must be confused."

Miriam picks up another parcel and turns it over in her hands. "Yes," she says. "Yes, he must."

*

Carl sat opposite his two children in the Hounds and Horses pub in Fishwick. He usually spent Friday nights with them and this time he felt like splashing out on a meal out. He felt like he was finally getting somewhere with *The Last Letter* and this was his way of celebrating. He just wished the other two were in a better mood.

Indie had barely looked up from her phone since they arrived, and, after declaring the entire menu a "stodge fest", had ordered a side salad and proceeded to organize a meet-up with her friends immediately afterwards.

Alex was acting strangely too. When Carl had told him where they were going, he had been dead against it. "Why there? Why Fishwick? Why can't we go somewhere else?"

Carl thought the boy was just being difficult and saw no reason not to go to the pub with the best steak pie in the area, but when they arrived, Alex insisted they take a table right at the back of the pub, away from everyone else, and put up his hood, even though it was warm in there.

Carl chuckled at the excitable screams echoing from the soft play area just down the hall.

"Remember when you two used to go in there? Loved it, both of you."

Indie didn't even respond, her eyes fixed on the phone while her thumbs danced impossibly quickly across the screen.

"Remember, Alex?" Carl prodded. "You wet yourself in the ball pool that time?"

"I don't actually remember that," he said, his eyes darting all around the pub.

"Why not?" said Indie. "It was only last week."

Carl took a sip of his drink and sighed. They might not have remembered, but he did, and it really did feel like it happened only last week. "Daddy, watch this! Daddy, come down the slide with me!" Looking back, he couldn't believe he had ever complained about it. He would give anything to have that back.

Carlos left his weekly evening with his kids, his mind awhirl with worry. Indie was going to volunteer for President Peregrine's brain microchip and Alex, being an impressionable boy, was sure to do the same eventually. Carlos had to do something.

WHAT DO I DO, THOUGH?

Carl sat back in his chair and knew that last question was as much for him as it was his character.

Chapter Seventeen

It's Saturday morning when Willow asks me out on a date.

OK, OK, it's not a date. What even is a date? You go to the cinema or have nice food together, right? This isn't that. This is just an out-of-work trip. That's all it is.

So, basically, we're sitting in a couple of fold-up chairs on the towpath next to *Lola*. I have only just calmed down after last night's most terrifying trip to a pub in my entire life. Madge is propped up on my lap, gently purring as she kneads my thighs to make herself comfortable. We're on a break before we tackle our last two bags. Willow ducks into the boat and emerges with a couple of cheese sandwiches on plastic plates, along with some pickled onions her mum bought from the shop.

"I'm glad she likes you," Willow says as Madge settles down to sleep on my lap. "She's a good judge of character."

"What do you mean?" I ask, trying to balance the plate on the arm of the chair without disturbing the cat.

"She can tell if you're a good person," says Willow. She takes off her cap and shakes her hair until it falls around her shoulders. "If she's comfortable around you, you're all right."

I look down at Madge as her eyelids gently flutter closed. It would be absolutely awful timing if she suddenly shrieks, jumps up and claws me in the face.

"And what if you're a bad person?" I ask.

"She knows," says Willow. "She'll keep her distance, hiss, arch her back. She did that with my dad."

I glance at her. This is the first time she's properly mentioned her dad. Every time I have asked about him before, she's changed the subject or just not even bothered answering.

"So your dad's not a good person?" I ask.

Willow laughs without smiling. "You could say that. Anyway, what are you doing tomorrow?"

There she goes again, changing the subject. The Natural Order of Things. Well, the thing is, I don't have anything planned. And as weird as it sounds, I miss Willow already, even though I am still with her.

"Nothing," I say and shrug, trying to sound casual while taking a bite of the cheese sandwich made with ingredients nicked from my kitchen.

"Want to come for a cruise?" she asks, nodding at the boat.

"On there?" I ask, cluelessly.

"No, in a Bugatti," says Willow, socking my arm gently. "Yes, on there."

"Where to?" I ask.

Willow rolls her eyes. "Just around. If you don't want to, I have plenty of other friends I can ask."

"No, no, no," I say, all flustered. "That sounds good. I'll meet your mum, right?"

Willow shakes her head. "Mum works all day Sunday. She doesn't mind me taking the boat out for a spin, though."

"Is that even legal?" I ask.

Willow flicks my ear, not at all gently. "Why are

you such a wet quilt, Alex? Do you want to come on a super fun boat ride with me, or what?"

So that's why I'm now walking down the ramp to the towpath, ready for our "date" that most definitely isn't a date. I scraped the last of the hair product that Dad and I used to share, smothering it on my head, and brought a roll-on deodorant with me, just in case. I don't want to be smelly on a boat. Phone: *present*. Wallet: *present*. Deodorant: *present*.

Say this is a date. It's not, but let's just pretend it is. What happens on dates? It's not like I can walk her home after, is it? We're on her home. Come on, Alex, don't overthink. If you arrive all sweaty and stuttering, she's going to tell you to leave.

Madge is sunbathing on the roof. I lean over and run a hand down her back, mostly to try and calm myself down. She gives me a look, then goes back to her lazy ritual.

I hear a clunk from below deck and Willow appears. She's wearing a white sailor hat with a few strands of hair hanging loose.

"Morning!" she says, with a smile.

I get a weird feeling in my stomach. It's all

fluttery and tingly. I smile back. Then I realize I'm supposed to be saying something, so I blurt out the first thing that pops into my tiny brain.

"I like your hat."

"Good," Willow says, her smile growing. "Because you've got one too."

She reaches down and pulls up a pirate tricorne, complete with a cartoon skull and crossbones.

"Where did you even get that?"

"Yarrrr, I bested Captain Blackbeard for it," she growls, swishing an imaginary cutlass. "Now come on, landlubber, are ye climbing aboard or not?"

I climb aboard, where Willow plonks the pirate hat on my head and smashes it down over my carefully waxed hair.

"You've been showing me the ropes this week; now it's time for the tables to turrrrn!" she says.

I frown at her. "Are you going to talk like a pirate all day?"

"YARRRRR!" she roars, then turns a key in a grey box, which makes the boat shudder to life. Madge jumps to her feet and slinks along the roof over to us, where she then squeezes through our legs and inside, curling up on the floor by the table.

"Oh, by the way," says Willow, dropping back into her normal voice. "I'm going to need you to push off."

"But I just got here!" I said.

Willow laughs and whacks my shoulder. "You're wasted as a postman. You should be on stage. I mean *you need to untie that rope.*" She nods at a rope that keeps the boat tied to a metal knob sticking out of the ground.

"Oh, right," I say. "I can do that."

I get off the boat again and loosen the rope until it slips off the peg. "Now what?" I ask.

"Throw it here, ya scurvy dog!" says Willow.

I shrug and chuck the rope at the boat. Unfortunately, some of it dunks into the canal and Willow shakes her head like I'm a puppy that's just done a number two on her best rug.

"Coil it up first, lad," she grumbles.

After she finishes doing what I should have done, she stands with her hand on the boat wheel (which I will later find out is actually called a "helm") and looks at me.

"Are you coming back on, or what?"

There is a gap opening up between the edge of the towpath and the boat and I don't know if I'm going to be able to step or if it'll require a jump. Oh, what am I going to do?

"Well, come on, then!" says Willow.

The gap gets wider. Now or never. In a split second, I decide I can manage the step. I stretch across, planting my right foot on the boat, but that has the effect of pushing the boat further away and … *oh no*, I'm doing the splits!

The seams on my trousers are cracking under the strain. Surely they're going to split.

Willow leans against the railing and grabs both my hands, yanking me on board. Wow, she's strong.

"Am I going to regret inviting you out today?" Willow asks, squinting at me in the bright sun.

I shrug, trying to regain my composure. "Maybe."

Willow tuts and adjusts my pirate hat. "I thought as much."

With that, she turns back to the steering wheel and pulls it to the side, then pushes a smaller stick forward. The boat slowly glides through the water, away from the bank. Willow lets out a little whoop and taps the roof.

"Good girl, *Lola*! Let's go!"

Now, I've never been on a boat like this before.

In fact, I'm pretty sure the only boat I've ever been on was a ferry to Ireland when I was about six. All I can remember is the sea was really rough and pretty much everyone was throwing up. This is a lot calmer, at least.

We pass moored boats and dog walkers and joggers and old ladies in sports clothes walking quickly with their elbows pointing outwards. Every now and then we'll disappear into the cool, musty darkness of a tunnel, before reappearing in the sunlight.

I keep glancing over at Willow. She looks so happy, her hand clutching the steering stick and her chin tilted proudly upwards while the few free strands of her hair blow freely. Seeing her like that makes me feel happy too. She looks so worried so much of the time, but now it's like she's lighter. I wish I could find something that does that for me. Even when I'm gaming, I'm still worrying.

We go so far, I don't think I know where we are any more. Thankfully, we've gone in the opposite direction of home.

"Lock up ahead," says Willow, nodding at a huge wooden bar across the canal.

Is it weird that I'm quite excited about this? Like, I've seen locks in action before, and they're just a way for the canal to go higher or lower, but there's still something fun about them. As we get closer, I can see this one is a downward one. Willow moves the small stick back into the middle and the boat begins to slow.

"OK, Captain Jack Sparrow," says Willow. "Can I trust you to do this and get back on the boat without splitting yourself in half again?"

"Yeah," I say. "Of course you can."

Thankfully, this time it goes smoother, and with Willow yelling instructions from the boat, I turn cranks and push big poles until Willow has steered *Lola* into the lock and the gate is closed. I stand on the edge and watch the boat descend as the water spills out of the other side.

Willow looks over at me, smiling and shaking her head at the same time. "You stand and watch your bath water drain out with this much amazement?" she shouts over the rushing water.

I laugh. "No. I don't have baths!"

Willow wrinkles her nose.

"No, I mean I have showers!" I shout. "I wash. I'm very clean."

"Glad to hear it," said a man walking a dog behind me.

Back on board the boat, with the lock behind us, Willow pokes me in the side. "All right, we're nearly there."

"Nearly where? I thought we were just going for a ride."

"We are," says Willow. "I just have a little somewhere in mind, that's all."

The canal narrows and the sunlight is blotted out by overhanging trees on each side.

"It's quite creepy this way, isn't it?" I say.

Willow cocks an eyebrow at me. "Want me to hold your hand?"

Do I? Kind of. But I'm not going to admit that, am I? That would be ridiculous. Besides, she'd think I'm some kind of wimp. Madge comes out from inside the boat and curls herself around my legs.

"Oh, hi, Madge," I say, relieved at the distraction, and I lean down and run my fingertips across the smooth curve of her head.

"I think she likes it around here," says Willow. "Much better than home."

The trees become a little more sparse and the sun is peeking through, casting beams of light across us as we glide.

"Where is home, anyway?" I ask.

Willow sniffs. "You wouldn't know it. It's miles away."

"I might."

Willow gently pulls on the stick as the canal bends towards a tunnel. "Don't you like a bit of mystery in your life, Alex?"

I think about it. No, actually I don't. I liked things as they were, with me and Mum, Dad and Indie (I guess). And Spencer being home for the summer. And not having to be a postman. As I've said a million times, the Natural Order of Things. There is no room for mystery in the Natural Order of Things.

This tunnel is longer than I thought it would be. Darkness surrounds us. Willow flips a switch and a lamp illuminates a little way ahead of us. I can feel the dampness oozing off the walls and I shiver.

I've often heard about a light at the end of the tunnel. Usually it's something Mum says when she's going through a rough time at work, or if I'm moaning about school and the holidays are coming up. I don't think I've ever seen one in real life.

I think about how my plan for the summer is going. What is my light at the end of the tunnel?

Is it Dad getting into writing again? Will it be Dad finishing the book? Or Mum and Dad being in the same room together without arguing?

The light grows, sunlight spills in and in seconds, we're out. On my side of the boat, tree trunks are stacked in pyramid formations while further up, half-finished houses sit abandoned.

"Hold on to the tiller for me, will you?" says Willow.

"The what?"

Willow laughs. "You really are a landlubber." She slaps the steering stick. "This thing. Can you hold it for me?"

She must sense me worrying a little because she grips my arm and says, "It's literally a straight line, Alex. Madge could do it." She holds my hand. My eyes lock on to hers. Wow. Is she feeling the same electric pulse? Is that happening because I might possibly maybe potentially like her, or is the wiring faulty and we're being electrocuted? Willow grins mischievously and places my hand on the steering stick before disappearing inside the boat.

OK, no time to dwell on what just happened. I am now in charge of a vehicle. I've never driven anything before. Wait, do you *drive* a boat? Surely you sail it? But sailing a barge doesn't sound right. *Oh, shut up and concentrate.* I feel Madge rub herself against my legs again, but I can't move. I have to make sure I don't crash the boat and kill all of us.

Wait a second. Oh no. Around the bend way up ahead, another barge is coming our way. Is the canal even wide enough for both of us?

"Willow!" I call out.

"Hang on, I'm just finding something!"

Oh, how is that boat getting so much closer? Is it speeding? Is there a speed limit for barges? A family of ducks scatters to get out of their way. What a reckless driver!

"Willow!"

"I said hang on!"

We're going to collide, aren't we? How do you stop this thing? What did Willow do when we got to that lock? Do boats have brakes? It's getting closer. Should I steer towards the bank? If I do that, we might crash into the side. Oh God. *I am but a tiny twig on the shoulders of a mighty stream. I am but a tiny twig on the shoulders of a mighty stream.*

"Willow!"

"Relax, will you?"

The boat is right ahead. It's being driven by a red-faced man smoking a pipe. We're going to crash. We're going to crash. I screw my eyes shut and brace for impact.

"Yarrrr! Nice hat, shipmate!" I hear the man say.

I open my eyes and the boat has passed. It's only now I realize I'm still wearing the silly pirate hat.

"What's up?" says Willow, coming back up with a piece of paper in her hand.

"Nothing," I say, trying to sound casual. "Just wanted to ask you about what to do when another boat is coming."

Willow leans off the roof and turns to see the other boat disappearing towards the tunnel. "Well, you didn't smash into it, so looks like you did a pretty good job."

She squints at the piece of paper, then folds it up and puts it in the pocket of her jeans. "All right, we need to stop soon."

"You still haven't said what we're stopping for," I say.

"Just a little walk in the woods," she says, taking back control of the boat.

A walk in the woods? But we've been through

loads of woods on the way here. What's so special about these woods?

Wait a second. What if Willow is some kind of serial killer? What if she goes from town to town in her boat, luring victims to the woods where she kills and buries them? I glance over at her, her arm casually draped over the side, and her eyes hidden by her shades.

"Just a walk in the woods, Alex," she says again. "Nothing to worry about."

Hmm. That's exactly what a serial killer would say.

Willow slows down the boat and brings it to a stop outside some dense trees. Looks very dark and murdery in there.

She gives me the rope and a couple of pegs and sends me off the boat so I can "moor up". It's easy enough and after Willow checks that the boat's not going to come loose and drift away, we leave it behind.

Willow leads me up a path through the trees. I notice her take the piece of paper back out of her pocket, check it again, then put it back.

"What's on there?" I ask.

"Oh, just instructions."

"Instructions for a walk in the woods?"

"Yeah," she says, picking up the pace.

"Enough of this now," I say, surprising even myself.

Willow stops and spins around. "Enough of what?"

"All the secrecy."

A worm of shame burrows into my gut. It's not as if I don't have secrets of my own, is it?

"What do you mean?"

"Coming out here, to this specific part of the woods, with a secret piece of paper and not telling me where we're going. It's weird!"

Willow's lips clamp shut, then wobble a little. For a second, I think she's going to cry, but then she grunts with laughter.

"Sorry," she says. "It's just really hard to take you seriously in that hat."

It's only now I remember I'm still wearing the dorky pirate headwear, so I quickly snatch it off.

"OK, fine," she says, her eyes darkening. "I'm just looking for someone, that's all."

"Who could you be looking for here?" I ask, gesturing around at the woods. "Bigfoot?"

"It's actually an old friend," she replies. "Eve

Haunton, remember? I heard she moved out here and I wanted to see if it was true. Is that all right with you?"

I remember now. She had asked me about her, back when we first spoke.

"Well, yeah," I say. "Of course it is. But why didn't you just say that in the first place?"

"Oh, I'm sorry!" Willow clamps her hand across her chest. "I didn't know I had to run everything by you. I know I'm working for you in the week, but I didn't realize you're my boss on our day off too!"

The sharpness of her voice throws me off balance and I can't think of anything to say back.

"All right, come on," Willow goes on, softer now. "The house should be just up here."

I stay behind her as we follow the bumpy dirt path. A white-tailed rabbit bobs alongside me for a couple of seconds before disappearing into the thick grass.

The path winds through the tall trees until we arrive at a dusty single-lane road. Straight ahead there's a sharp curve leading to a set of huge iron gates, closed in on either side by barbed wire fencing. To my surprise, Willow heads straight for the gate.

"Your friend lives here?" I ask. "Is she in prison?"

Willow shakes her head. "No, it's just secure." She presses a buzzer on the side of the gate and the little speaker underneath lets out a long beep. Willow chews on her thumbnail.

BEEEEEEEEEP.
BEEEEEEEEEP.
BEEEEEEEEEP.

"Hello, reception?" a crackly voice finally emerges.

"Yeah, hi. Is Eve Haunton there?" says Willow, removing her thumb from her mouth.

It goes quiet for a second, then the crackle returns. "I'm afraid I can't give out information about residents over the intercom."

Willow lets out an exasperated sigh. "Well, how about over the phone?"

"I can't do that, either."

Willow looks at me like she expects me to help, but then her eyes flicker and she looks at the ground. "So, you can't even tell me if Eve is a resident or not?"

"Sorry, I can't," says the voice.

"Is there no way I can find out?" says Willow, her eyes closed.

“No,” says the voice. “The person, if they are a resident, has to get in touch with you.”

“But I...” Willow stops and touches her fingertips to her lips. “OK, thank you.”

With that, she turns and stomps away, back to the road.

A flash of red, a crunch, a squeal.

“WILLOW!”

The car skids to a stop centimetres away from Willow. She stands and stares at the windscreen, shaking.

The driver leans out of the window. “What the hell do you think you’re doing, you silly girl? I almost killed you!”

Willow turns and runs back into the woods. The driver shakes his head at me, then carries on.

I have to sprint to catch up with Willow. “What happened back there?” I ask.

“I don’t want to talk about it,” she replies, her jaw clenched tight. She picks up the pace and rubs her eyes with her palm. I think she’s crying, and it makes my skin prickle all over. I want to fix things, but I don’t even know what the problem is.

We get back to the boat and Willow quickly

unmoors it herself and jumps on, starting the engine straight away. I jump on behind her and just make it.

She doesn't speak all the way home, and my every attempt to start a conversation is met with silence or grunts.

We get to Fishwick and I'm about to leave when she calls me back.

"Sorry about today," she says, staring at her battered trainers.

"That's OK," I say. "It was fun."

"We both know it wasn't, Alex."

We look at each other. A light breeze skitters across the surface of the canal.

"Are you going to be OK?" I ask.

Willow nods and rubs her nose with the back of her hand. "I just miss my friend, that's all."

I understand that. I'm kind of missing Spencer too. Even though he is super annoying.

"Before you go," she says, "can I borrow your phone? I only need it for like two minutes."

I reach into my pocket and hand it over, slightly panicking about what I've left on there. When we first met properly, I had searched her name on all the social networks I could think of, but came up with nothing. Not a surprise really, since I only know her first name.

Willow frowns as she taps into my phone. I stand by with my hands in my pockets. I want to know what she's doing, but I'm too scared to ask.

After a couple of minutes, she gives it back with a sigh. "Thanks, Alex. See you tomorrow."

When I'm over the bridge and down the road, I check the search history. Sure enough, there is the name "Eve Haunton".

President Peregrine

Carlos spent the last of his savings on a ticket to the capital, where President Peregrine was giving a speech outside the palace. The square was thronged with crowds, and Carlos had to jostle through to get a good view of him.

Carlos has only seen the president on TV, and in real life he was just as loathsome: a tiny tyrant, puffed up on his own ego. Carlos wanted nothing more than to rush the stage and take him down, but he knew he would never get past the guards who prowled the perimeter, armed to the teeth.

With the speech over, Peregrine was whisked away in a reinforced black car and Carlos was left standing uselessly in the adoring crowd. He wanted to shake people and say, "Can't you see what this man wants to do to us? We need to fight back!" But he knew no one would. Nobody cared about what happened in the Badlands, and they would never believe that it would come for them. But it would. It would come for us all.

Carlos was determined that this wouldn't be a wasted journey. He had to stop Peregrine. But how?

Yeah, Carl thought, leaning back on the creaking sofa. *How?* It's not like you could just climb in through the window of the White House or 10 Downing Street and have a word with the guy in charge, could you? It was bad enough trying to speak to the actual Peregrine when you had a problem, shutting himself away in his office, always on his headset phone talking about volume figures.

Carl was going to have to think creatively if he was going to solve this one. Or maybe ask for advice. Alex was always playing those computer games where you have to do complicated missions. He could have some tips for him.

Carl called Alex, always at the top of his contacts. After two attempts, Alex finally answered.

"Hi, Dad," he said, sounding out of breath, almost like he was walking up a big hill.

"Hi, Alex. I was wondering if you could help me with the book?"

"Oh," said Alex. "What's the matter?"

"Well, there's this bit where the main character needs to get to the president, and—"

"Actually, Dad, could I call you back later?" Alex cut in. "Can't really talk at the moment."

Carl sighed. "Sure. Talk to you later."

There had been a time when Carl's son would never have been too busy to talk to him. They had been like best friends.

Carl rubbed his tired eyes and stared at the screen until the words became black spidery blurs. An idea began to form in his mind. Alex might have just given him the answer without intending to...

Chapter Eighteen

I quickly end my call with Dad and put my phone away as I see Willow bounding down the hill with her hands clasped behind her back.

"Heyyy!" she says.

Her cheerfulness is like a rainbow after a storm for me, after having spent the morning in the depot with Lloyd and Miriam, who barely spoke to each other the entire time. I think they had a row about something before I arrived.

"Brought you a present," she says, bringing her hands to the front and holding out an open palm. Lying on it is a flat rock, on which she's painted a postbox with my name above it in big orange letters. It looks amazing, like it was professionally printed, and I blush so hard there's probably no blood left in the rest of my body.

"Wow," I say. "Thanks, Willow."

She shrugs like it's nothing. "I'm into arts and crafts, so it didn't take long."

"Well, it's really nice," I say, carefully picking it up and examining it closer, marvelling at the tiny, delicate brushstrokes, hoping that studying it will disguise how badly I continue to blush.

"Also, it's to say sorry," she says. "I was kind of a jerk yesterday."

I haven't been able to stop thinking about what happened. It was all so weird. Why is she so desperate to find this friend? And why does she think her friend lives in this super secure place in the middle of nowhere?

"Oh," I say. "Well, thanks. I wish you'd let me help you, though."

"Let's just forget about it, eh?" she says, sharply. "Start a new week fresh?"

I nod. "OK, sounds good." It's obvious she doesn't want my help. Which stings, if I'm honest.

Willow sniffs. "All right, enough of this gooey nonsense. Let's get to work, shall we?"

*

"ALEX, DINNER!"

My eyes shoot open. Mum is standing over my bed, hands on hips. I'm so shocked I think my soul has left my body. I sit up and smack my dry mouth.

"What time is it?"

"Nearly seven," says Mum. "You've been asleep since I came home from work. Are you feeling all right?"

She leans over and holds her hand to my forehead.

"I'm fine," I grumble, shaking her off. "Just tired, that's all."

"Well, tired or not, I want you straight downstai—" She stops mid-word and stares at my side. I follow her gaze and realize too late that it's the rock Willow painted for me.

"What's that?" asks Mum, half-frowning and half-smiling.

My heart thuds and my head buzzes. I'm wide awake now. "Oh, that's, that's … I did that."

Mum laughs so suddenly and violently, it sounds more like a fart. "Pull the other one, son, I've seen your art book from school and you can't paint like that."

I scoop up the rock, throw open my sock

drawer and drop it in there. "Well, I've been practising."

Mum rolls her eyes. "I bet you have. Well, if you're not going to tell me why some mystery person is painting your name on stones with postboxes for some reason, then I suppose I'll just have to draw my own conclusions."

Why didn't I hide it when I got in? I need to be more careful.

I sit on the edge of my bed and rub my eyes. "Just forget it, all right?"

When we get downstairs, Indie is already sitting at the table, picking at her side salad. It's fish tonight. I hate fish. Always having to pull little bones out of your mouth? No thanks.

When Indie sees me, she grins. It makes my stomach turn. She never smiles at me unless she's about to make me miserable.

"What were you two talking about?" she asks, in this annoying sing-song voice.

Mum sits down and spreads a napkin across her lap, just like she always does. "Alex has a lovely rock with his name on it."

"Do not," I huff. "Shut up, will you?"

"Manners!" Mum warns. "Anyway, it's really

sweet. You should be grateful someone likes you enough to make you something like that."

Indie gasps, her mouth a perfect shape of evil. "Oh my God, I think I know who made that!"

I scowl at her and try to hide how nervous she's making me. "What are you talking about?"

"It was Lola, wasn't it?"

I feel like my ears have flattened against my head, like a scared dog. "I don't know anyone called Lola," I say, which is technically not a lie.

Indie slides her phone to our side of the table. There's a photo on there and I feel sick.

I scramble to pick up the phone, but Mum beats me to it. I try and grab it off her, but she holds it out of my reach.

"I hate you so much," I hiss at Indie.

I only got a quick glimpse of the photo, but I could tell what it was. It's of me and Willow standing on the boat. It looks like it was taken from the bridge. Willow is pressing the pirate hat down on my head.

"What are you, like the paparazzi or something?" I growl.

Indie giggles. "I was just on my way to Grace's house," she says. "How was I to know my baby brother was going to be smooching a barge girl?"

"WE WERE NOT SMOOCHING!" I yell.

"Stop it, you two," says Mum, squinting at the phone in that "I don't have my glasses" way of hers. "She looks lovely, Alex. What's her name?"

"She's just a friend," I huff, trying to will my raging blush to go down.

"Justafriend?" says Mum. "That's a strange name."

I groan and lean back in my chair. I can see they're not going to let this go. I'd better just give them the information they're asking for. It's easier that way.

"Willow," I say.

"OOOOOOOOOOH!" they both coo as if from a script.

"That's a beautiful name," says Mum.

"Yeah, very Earth Child," says Indie, throwing up a peace sign.

"So what's her story?" Mum asks. "Is she on a boating holiday and just stopping over?"

"Something like that," I say.

Mum gasps. "A holiday romance. Oh, I remember mine."

I clamp my hands over my ears, but I can still hear the odd word. "Kiss. Tenerife. Kevin." It makes me want to vomit.

When I'm sure she's stopped, I take my hands away and cut off a piece of fish. It's moments like this I really miss Dad at home. He would have seen I was embarrassed and changed the subject. He did it for me loads. It was the Natural Order of Things. Now I'm outnumbered.

"Well, when you see Willow next, you tell her she's officially invited to dinner."

Are you kidding me? My mind whizzes with all the possible downfalls that would happen if Willow were to meet Mum and Indie. She'd tell them I'm working as a postman straight away. Game over.

"I'm not going to do that," I say. "She's just a friend."

"Well, Spencer is your friend and he comes around for dinner all the time," says Mum.

"And he doesn't paint you lovely rocks," says Indie, making disgusting kissy noises.

"You know what?" I say, standing up and picking up my plate. "I'm eating this upstairs."

"Alex," says Mum, that warning tone back.

"Let him go, Mum," says Indie. "He probably

wants to go up and tell Willow their secret romance has been rumbled."

"THERE IS NO ROMANCE!" I yell.

Mum and Indie laugh.

"Sure there isn't," says Indie. "Bike rides, indeed."

I stomp upstairs and slam my bedroom door behind me. That might have been the most embarrassing dinner of my life. The only upside is at least it might throw Indie off the scent of why I'm really leaving early every morning.

Ugh. When did everything get so complicated?

Chapter Nineteen

"Where are you off so early?"

The voice startles me as I leave the house and I nearly fall off my bike.

Dad stands on the path by our drive, grinning. I can see he's had a shave and combed his hair. He's starting to look a bit younger. Like the rest is recharging him.

"Oh, just out for a bike ride," I say, knowing he won't laugh at it like the others.

Dad chuckles and hucks me on the arm. "I bet you are, you old dog."

"What are you talking about?" I say. I glance at my watch. If he keeps me talking much longer, I'm going to be late.

"That girlfriend of yours," he says. "What's her

name, Ivy?"

"It's Willow," I correct him. "And she's not my girlfriend."

"'Course she isn't," he says, with an annoying wink.

"How do you even know about that, anyway?" I ask.

"Hey, just because your mother and I are separated, it doesn't mean we don't co-parent. She still keeps me up to date with what's going on."

Oh, lucky me!

"What are you doing here this early?" I say, keen to change the subject. "It's six in the morning."

"Come with me," he says, then turns towards his car, parked a little way up the road. He presses the "open boot" button on his key fob a few times, but it doesn't work, so he tuts and opens it with his hands, revealing his secret: a couple of fishing rods and a tub of bait.

"How about it, son? Want to come fishing with your old man?"

I look up at Dad's face, smiling big. I can't go. I know I can't. But how am I going to get out of it?

"Fishing?" I say.

"Yeah, I know we haven't been in years, but I

thought we could start again? A new father-son tradition."

I remember the few times we've been before. We never really caught much, besides one big fish, but it was still fun. Dad would blast his rubbish music on his crackly speakers and we'd swap jokes and funny stories. I don't hate the idea of going fishing, but obviously it can't happen. Not today, at least.

I blink hard and take a deep breath. "I can't."

Dad shakes his head with a little snigger. "You can be apart from your girlfriend for one day, can't you?"

"She's not my girlfriend," I say. "And anyway, it's not that."

"Well, what is it, then?"

I look at the houses on the other side of the street as if I'll find the answer there.

"Shouldn't you be writing your book?" I ask, stalling for time.

Dad puts his hands on his hips, squeezing the fleshy parts above his belt. "I'm allowed the odd day off, you know," he says. "Besides, being in the outdoors will be good inspiration. And a *certain person* forgot to call me back the other day to help me."

I close my eyes. Oh yeah. I did forget, didn't I? I

was just so tired after work that it slipped my mind. But I can't go with him. Not now.

Think of something, Alex. Think, think, think. You can't not go into work. The stuff has to be delivered, and Miriam and Lloyd will be worried. And who are they going to call to ask where I am? Dad, of course.

"OK, so it is Willow," I say. "Kind of. You see, we're, uh, doing volunteer work."

Dad stares at me boggle-eyed, like I've just told him I'm building a rocket and blasting off to explore the surface of the sun.

"What kind of volunteer work?"

Think of something, fluffbrain. You pretty much already are doing volunteer work. This actually isn't that much of a lie.

"Charity shop," I say.

"Which one?"

My brain desperately scrambles for the name of a charity shop, and Dad is staring at me, his forehead creased and his lips pursed. "Save the Cats," I blurt out.

Dad's expression doesn't change. "'Save the Cats'?"

"Something like that," I say. "Something to do

with cats."

I don't feel quite as bad about lying because I have a tin of tuna I swiped from the kitchen in my bag and it's going to be for Madge, so in a way, I am actually saving a cat.

Dad juts out his chin and bobs his head. "All right, son, I'll go fishing by myself."

My stomach twists. This is horrible. "We'll go some other time, OK?"

"Sure," says Dad. "I was trying to surprise you, but I need to understand you're a young man now. You've got your own life going on." He ruffles my hair. "My little dude's growing up."

I close my eyes and sigh. In order to save my family, I'm having to pie my dad off. There's something backwards about this.

"Sorry, Dad," I say.

He squeezes my shoulder. "You don't have to apologize to me, OK? Just make sure you save all those cats."

Carl sank into his fold-up chair by the canal and watched the line. It had been years since he'd been fishing. His tackle was in the loft at the old house and he couldn't face the arguments with Kate, so he'd borrowed Pete's. It was much fancier than his anyway. Sandra insisted on knowing exactly where he was going, but he told her the wrong location. He couldn't have her showing up at his peaceful fishing spot with another vicar.

This was the place he always used to come with Alex, just a little down from the bridge, all covered in creeping vines. It wasn't as quiet as it used to be. A few years ago it was wild nature – shoulder-height grass, gnarled trees – but now, a little way down, diggers were churning up the earth to lay the foundations for a new housing estate.

Carl didn't like it. He knew people needed places to live, but he couldn't help think about what humanity was losing, and what it was heading towards. What would happen when there were no more green spaces like this?

He checked the line again. Still nothing. Last time he was here with Alex, they had caught a big carp. The size of his arm, it had been. He still had the photo somewhere. He got out his phone and tried to scroll back and find it, but he couldn't.

Carl opened the Notes app. He could get a bit of *The Last Letter* down while he was waiting for a bite.

Carlos had been sitting on the same bar stool for so many hours, he couldn't even begin to guess how many.

"Another," he grunted to the grizzled bartender, who was shining a glass with a filthy rag and his spit.

The bar door squeaked open and an old man shambled in. Carlos could smell him from where he was. His straggly grey beard was matted and clogged with the memories of week-old fried breakfasts.

"No, no, no," the bartender barked. "Get outta here, Lloyd. You're banned, remember?"

"Because I speak the truth about this so-called president?" the old man said.

Now that got Carlos's attention. He turned and looked at this Lloyd properly for the first time. He noticed he was missing the end of his right index finger. How did that happen?

"No, because you're stubborn as a mule and twice as stinky," said the bartender. "And you still haven't paid your tab."

The old man folded his arms. "And what if I'm

here to pay my tab?"

"Are you?" said the bartender.

Lloyd frowned at the neon signs above the bar for a few seconds. "No."

The barman slammed his glass down. "THEN GETOUTTAHERE!"

Lloyd turned and kicked the door open, cursing loudly the whole way. Carlos knew he could have just been some cantankerous old man, but what if he wasn't?

Carlos threw some cash on the bar and followed Lloyd out into the dark alleyway.

"Hey!"

The old man slowly turned around and looked Carlos up and down. "I don't want any trouble, mister."

"Neither do I," said Carlos. "What you said back there, about you knowing the truth about Peregrine?"

Lloyd narrowed his watery eyes at Carlos. "Yeah?"

"Is it the microchips?"

Lloyd's weathered face broke out into a smile. "Come with me, my friend. I'll show you what I know."

Carl tried to imagine Lloyd's lab. He was going to be a former employee of the president, something like a scientific advisor, but he would have left in protest at his outrageous plans. What would be in his lab? Would it be neat and tidy to contrast his messy appearance? Or would it be chaotic and unhygienic? He closed his eyes to help himself think, but soon thinking became dreaming, and he fell sound asleep in his chair.

Chapter Twenty

After work, Willow invites me down to the boat for lunch. We have cheese toasties and crisps while Madge greedily guzzles down the entire tin of tuna in about ten seconds.

"So," I say, relaxing into the deck chair and enjoying the sun on my face, "have you managed to find out any more about your friend?"

Willow shakes her head while her mouth works on the toastie. "Dead end," she says, all muffled. Before I can say anything else, she gets up and heads inside the boat, returning a few seconds later with that same rope and magnet gadget she saved my trolley with that day we first met.

"Anyway, I thought we could have a go at this," she says.

*

We walk a little further up the towpath and stop just the other side of a bridge.

"You can sometimes find good stuff in here," she says, uncoiling the rope. "Scrap yard will pay for stuff that's not too damaged. Me and Mum found a safe once. It was empty, but it fetched a few quid."

Willow casts the rope out into the canal. The magnet hits the water with a splash and sinks beneath the surface. Willow waits for a while then pulls, but the magnet re-emerges with nothing. She tries again, but still no luck.

"Let's move up a bit."

As we pass under the bridge, a rat scurries in front of us and I freeze in my tracks.

Willow giggles. "Scared?"

"No," I say, even though I definitely am. Rats have always given me the creeps.

"Why? It's only a vole," says Willow.

"Wait, so it's not a rat?"

Willow shakes her head as the creature disappears into a hedge.

"Well, what's the difference?"

"Chubbier body, smaller tail," she replies. "I think they're cute. Then again, rats are too."

"Really?"

We stop a little way ahead of where the vole vanished and Willow hands the rope to me.

"Of course. I'm guessing you don't agree?"

I shiver a little. "No."

Willow laughs and bites down on her bottom lip, flesh oozing under her broken tooth. I really like that broken tooth. Is that weird?

"But I bet you don't mind squirrels?" she says.

"Not really."

"So, really, what you like is fluffy tails," she chuckles. "Anyway, your go now. Just chuck it in, but for crying out loud, remember to hang on to the rope."

I try and remember what she did back there and toss the magnet into the middle of the canal. The rope burns my hands a little as it sinks. I could be mistaken, but I thought I felt a little *clunk* on the line. I try and pull, but whatever it's attached to doesn't budge.

"I think I've got a big one!" I say, which is something I've heard those annoying blokes on those fishing documentaries Dad watches say.

"Oh yeah?" says Willow. "Let me give you a hand."

Willow grabs the rope further down and starts helping me heave it in, bracing herself against the edge of the towpath.

We pull and pull until something shiny breaks the surface and heads towards us like a shark's fin.

"Keep going!" Willow says through the strain. "We're almost there!"

Something lands on the bank with a wet thud, and I'm falling backwards thanks to the momentum. My foot catches something and I'm on my back, all the wind knocked out of me. *Ouch.*

Above me, Willow's laughing face is framed by the clear blue sky.

"You all right down there?"

I wheeze something that sounds like, "No."

"Want to see your big catch?"

I drag some air into my lungs and scramble to my feet. I hope what I think I saw coming out of the water is something else, something useful, but no, I was right. It's just a grimy shopping trolley.

"Ta-da!" Willow holds out her hands like a magician's assistant.

"So I take it it's not worth much money?"

"Not really," she replies. "Unless they've left the pound in it."

We move further up the canal and try again, but the best thing we manage to find is a rusty scooter.

Willow shakes her head and looks out at the canal. "There's something big down there, I just know it."

We head back to the boat, where Madge greets us both with leg rubs. I hear clanking coming from the tunnel behind me, followed by a long thin scrape, as if something is dragging along the roof. I turn around to see what it is … but it's too late to hide. He's already seen me.

"Alex!" Dad yells, bounding towards us, weighed down by fishing bags.

Willow looks at me with a questioning expression, but before I can explain, Dad booms, "Fancy seeing you here, son!"

It's only when he's standing close that I notice there's something off about him. It takes me a second, but then it clicks. "Oh my … what happened to your face?"

"What about my face?" he asks.

What about it? It's the colour of a beetroot! And to make things worse, there are two white circles around his eyes where his sunglasses must have been. Dad gets out his phone and looks at himself.

"Oh dear," he chuckles. "I may have fallen asleep in the sun for a while there. Wait a second – where are my manners?" He drops his bags on the floor and holds out a hand.

"I'm Carl, Alex's dad," he says. "You must be Willow, his girlfriend."

"She is NOT my girlfriend!" I moan.

Willow shakes Dad's hand while shooting me a look. "You don't have to sound so horrified, Alex."

"I didn't mean it like that," I exclaim. "It's just … it's just … I don't know what it's just."

Dad laughs and ruffles my hair, even though he knows I hate it. "Always has been a smooth talker, this one. He gets it from his old man."

Willow rolls her eyes. "He's right, though, I'm not his girlfriend. Heaven forbid!"

"So where did you two meet, then?" asks Dad.

"At work!" I yell, before Willow can say anything. "At our voluntary job."

Willow side-eyes me. "Well, not really."

"Yes! That's where we met. At our voluntary job. Anyway, Dad, we have to go!"

"We?" says Dad, his giant red face crinkling. "You coming back to mine, then?"

"Yep!" I say, my voice still super loud. "I want to see how this book is coming along. See you later, Willow!"

I walk away with Dad, helping him with his bags.

I think I might have got away with that one.

Chapter Twenty-One

"So are you going to tell me why you were acting so weird in front of your dad last night?" Willow asks as soon as she arrives on the hill. She's wearing a black T-shirt that's too big for her and jeans with holes in the knees. I don't remember seeing her in those clothes before. Not that I have time to ask her about it, because she's clearly not happy.

I open the trolley and pretend to be confused by something in there. I'm not. Everything is in perfect order, as it always is. I'm just stalling for time. *What am I supposed to say?*

"Hello?"

OK, turns out stalling for time doesn't work with Willow. I peer up at her from the open lid. "I wasn't acting weird, was I?"

Willow goes up on her tiptoes and holds out her arms at an odd angle from her body, a gormless look spreading across her face: dull eyes, slack mouth.

"DUUUUH! I MET HER AT MY VOLUNTARY JOB! SHE'S NOT MY GIRLFRIEND!"

"Hang on, is that supposed to be me?"

"DUUUUH!"

A car glides up the hill and comes to a stop next to us. I'm used to this, people asking me for directions just because I'm carrying a postbag. The amount of people I must have sent the wrong way these past few weeks is probably astronomical.

I plaster on my best helpful smile and turn towards the car, only for my smile to disappear just as fast. There, sitting in a Barson's Estate Agency car, the window rolled down, is Mum, beaming at us.

"Hello, you! What are you doing hanging around your dad's trolley?"

I rush over to the car. "Oh, nothing, just come out for a walk."

I sense Willow's presence next to me. Why did she have to come over too? And why did Mum have to turn up? What are the odds?

"What are you talking about?" Willow asks me.

Tentacles of fear grip my ribcage. This can't happen. Not here, not now.

"Oh, hello, my love!" says Mum. "You must be Willow."

"I am," she replies. "Not his girlfriend, though! Just saying it before he does."

Mum looks confused for a second, then shakes her head quickly and smiles again. "Well, it's so nice to finally meet you. I must say, the rock you painted for Alex was quite lovely."

"Thanks," says Willow. "And nice to meet you too."

Mum narrows her eyes at us, still smiling. "I can't stay long, I've got a viewing in the village in five, but it would be lovely to properly meet you. Would you like to come over for dinner tonight?"

The tentacles grow stronger, their grip tightening until I can hardly breathe. I need to say something to discourage this. Something smooth. Something that will work but won't offend anyone.

"NOOOOOOO!" I yell.

Well done, brain. Excellent work.

Mum and Willow both glare at me.

"I'm so sorry, Willow," says Mum. "I raised him to be much more polite than that."

"But … but she can't."

"Why not?" they both say simultaneously.

Because if she does, my entire plan will come crashing down? Because she will tell Mum I've been doing Dad's job all summer? Because the Natural Order of Things will be obliterated for ever? That kind of thing?

"I'd love to come for dinner," says Willow, with a sweet smile. "Thank you very much."

"So it's settled," says Mum. "It'll be ready at about six thirty. See you then, my love!"

And with that, Mum drives away.

Willow scowls at me so hard it feels like she's going to burn a hole in my face with her eyes.

"Hello," I say, weakly.

"Explain." She says it so sharply I can hear the full stop.

"Expla—"

"Don't lie to me," she says. "Tell me why you're acting so weird around your parents. Why don't you want them knowing about me? Are you ashamed of me because I live on a boat?"

The tentacles of terror become tentacles of guilt. "No! Please don't say that! It's just, I…"

I could tell her everything, the entire plan. When

I think of it in my head, it makes perfect sense, but when I try and put it into words, it collapses like a matchstick tower. I imagine saying the words, and I see her laughing at me. Thinking I'm a complete weirdo.

"Mum doesn't know I have this job, OK?"

Willow looks at me like I'm speaking Jupitese. "What? Why?"

The guilt gets worse. I close my eyes and hope for the best. "She wanted me to get this proper office job for my work experience. I didn't apply in time and ended up getting this instead. If she finds out, she'll hit the roof."

I open my eyes. I hate lying. Willow looks a little softer now. At least like she no longer wants to murder me.

"Your mum doesn't seem that strict," she says.

"She is, though," I say. "So, please, when you come to dinner, don't say anything about this job."

Willow sighs. "You and your family are weird, Alex."

I can't really argue with that, can I?

The Machine

“Wait a second,” said Carlos, rubbing his forehead. “Can you run that by me again? I’m confused.”

Lloyd had expected that. But everyone he had spoken to about this had outright dismissed him, so he was relieved to finally have someone actually believe him.

“Peregrine will have a microchip in the head of everyone in this country within a year,” said Lloyd. “And once he’s done that, he’ll be president for life. Everyone will do his bidding.”

“And you’re saying the only way to stop him is to—”

“Travel back in time,” said Lloyd, as if it were the most normal thing in the world.

Carlos rolled his tense shoulders and swallowed hard. It sounded preposterous, but he said it as though it was completely plausible. His eyes were full of sincerity.

“Say that’s even possible,” said Carlos. “Then what?”

Lloyd stepped closer to Carlos, his voice low and even. “We go back to a time before Peregrine was president, and we stop him.”

Lloyd moved over to a shiny steel machine in the corner, about the size of a phone box. There was a small door on the side, which he opened by turning a dial.

"This is it," he said. "This is how we bring down Peregrine."

Carl sat back and admired his handiwork. It was starting to come together. He didn't think there would be time travel in this novel, but he was excited to see where it went. He decided to watch some time travel movies. For research purposes, of course. Right after he rubbed some aftersun lotion into his face.

Chapter Twenty-Two

"You should be honoured, Willow," says Indie. "We don't usually get the fancy stuff."

She has a point, for a change. Mum has put an actual tablecloth down and we're eating from our "best plates". In other words, the ones that normally only get used at Christmas. The food is next level too, with our plates piled high with chilli, rice and homemade wedges. Willow must be enjoying it because she's shovelling it in like there's no tomorrow. I'm sitting opposite her. Mum made nameplates and everything.

"It'd be nice to get to meet your mum at some point over the summer, Willow," says Mum.

Willow swallows and dabs at her mouth with her napkin. "Yeah, it would. Problem is, she's always busy. Work, work, work, you know how it is."

"Oh really?" says Mum. "What does she do?"

"She's got, like, three jobs," says Willow. "Cleaning, working in a shop, and in a pub at night." Then she goes back to eating. I feel Mum's eyes on me, but I don't acknowledge it. I just want to get tonight over with as soon as possible. I love spending time with Willow, but not with my family. It's far too stressful.

"I've, um, got some more, if you want, Willow?" says Mum, nodding at her now empty plate.

"That'd be great, thanks!" Willow replies.

Mum takes Willow's plate and heads into the kitchen. Indie puts her phone down and looks from me to Willow. Here we go.

"So is it just your mum you live with, Willow?" Indie asks.

Willow nods. "Just the two of us. Well, three with our cat, Madge."

"And is your dad not around?"

"Indie!" I say. "Why are you so nosy?"

She reaches over and flicks my ear, which really stings. "Our dad isn't around either, Alexander. I'm just trying to establish common ground with our guest."

"But our dad *is* around," I protest. "He just lives at Uncle Pete's."

"I haven't seen him in a long time," says Willow. "And he's nothing like your dad. Your dad is nice."

"Oh," says Indie, who seems to be thinking about something now. Maybe she's realizing that Dad isn't so bad after all? Then again, knowing her she's probably just had another idea for her next terrible poem.

The table remains quiet until Mum re-emerges with another plate of chilli and wedges, which Willow begins to demolish. Mum watches for a second but doesn't sit down.

"Actually, Alex, could you help me with something in the kitchen?" she finally says.

I groan. "What could I possibly help you with in there?"

"Something that requires strength," says Mum. "You're the man of the house now after all." She blasts me with this annoying wink.

Willow laughs through a mouthful of chilli. "I don't know about that. You should have seen him trying to work a lock."

In the kitchen, Mum shuts the door behind

us and stands opposite me, leaning against the counter with her arms wrapped around herself.

"I know you've been taking food from the kitchen, Alex," she says.

I go to protest, but she holds up a hand. "I'm not angry, OK? I just need to know that everything's all right."

"What do you mean?" I ask, my cheeks flushing.

"I mean Willow," she says. "Why is she so hungry? Is she being looked after?"

"Of course she is, she lives with her mum," I say.

"And have you seen her mum?"

I think for a second. I haven't. She's always at work. But if I tell Mum that, I know exactly what will happen: she'll get nosier, she'll ask more questions, she'll snoop around. And if she does that, she'll get closer to finding out about my secret job. This morning was close enough as it is.

"Yes," I say. "She's nice. And I only take food for us to have at lunchtime, that's all."

Mum smiles, but it doesn't reach her eyes. "Fine, but if you find out Willow is in any trouble, any trouble at all, you have to tell me, OK?"

I nod. "OK."

Chapter Twenty-Three

I have the depot to myself now that Miriam and Lloyd have left. It's getting easier now. I know where everything goes and I've done it so many times, I barely have to think about it: mail in slots, parcels on shelves, redirections, leaflets, band up, bag up. Boom, boom, boom. Methodical. Systematic. This is actually the perfect job for me, in a way.

I'm just placing the parcels into the last bag when I hear a car or van pull up outside. I know it's not Miriam and Lloyd coming back. Their van makes a whining noise I instantly recognize. This sounds … *smaller*. Who could it be? I climb on to a chair and look out of the grimy window high up on the wall. Squinting through the green haze, I see a big car driven by a small man.

I jump down from the chair so quickly I roll my ankle. It hurts, but I have no time to limp. *I've got to get out of here!* There's only one way in and out of this depot. *Oh no, I'm going to have to hide!* I dive across the room and into the toilet, slamming and locking the door behind me.

Oh man, it stinks in here. I've managed to get through the past three weeks without having to use it. I normally wait until I'm out on the round and go to the café.

The main door opens and footsteps echo. I soundlessly step backwards until the backs of my legs are touching the disgusting toilet.

"Carl?" Peregrine hoots.

This can't be happening. He's here for Dad?!

"Carl, are you here?"

BANG, BANG, BANG.

"Are you in the gents, Carl?"

"Carl?"

The door handle turns and the flimsy lock rattles.

"If no one is in there, then why is the door locked?"

The handle turns again. I hear him sigh, then there's a rustling sound. Now there's something else.

Brrrrrr brrrrr. Brrrrrr brrrrr.

That's… *Oh no, he's calling someone.* He must be calling Dad! I can't breathe, this is not happening, this is not happening. That's it. Game over. I'm going to prison.

Brrrrrr brrrrr. Brrrrrr brrrrr. Brrrrrr brrrrr. Brrrrrr brrrrr.

Peregrine sighs again. "Yeah, hey, Carl. I attended the depot this morning and found your round half-prepped and you nowhere to be found. Plus, the toilet door seems to be banjaxed. Anyway, I have some paperwork about the Greenwood sitch, and I need you to confirm that it is accurate and that you stand by your assertion that you and only you have been delivering his mail. I look forward to your response."

I breathe again. Dad didn't answer. That was a voicemail message. As soon as I hear Peregrine leave and his car pull away, I leap back out of the bathroom, on to my bike and pedal as fast as I can down the canal towpath. Thankfully, Willow is still inside the boat so I don't have to stop and explain myself.

I have to get to Dad's phone before he picks up that message.

"MORNING, YOUNG MAN!" Brenda yells from the bridge. "YOU SHOULD SLOW DOOOOWN."

But I can't take Brenda's advice. There's no time. I duck under bridges, I dodge jagged rocks sticking out of the ground and my legs burn. I can normally make it to Dad's in ten minutes. Let's see if I can do it in five.

I speed up the ramp and on to the main road. There's an old bloke walking his dogs, so I hop off the curb and stick to the side of the road. Maybe Dad is still in bed. Maybe he hasn't even looked at his phone?

"Oh, hello!" says Auntie Sandra as I hurtle down her garden path, abandoning my bike. "Why are you in such a hurry?"

"Have to speak to Dad!" I half-shout, half-pant over my shoulder.

"That's good!" I hear her yell after me. "He needs to talk!"

I find the door to Dad's annexe open. That means he's up. That is not good news.

I step inside quietly and listen for telltale signs. If he's angry, he'll be pacing around, maybe even stomping. But I can't hear anything. Wait a second – yes, I can. There's a light tapping noise coming from the kitchen. I head down the hall and find Dad sitting at the counter, hunched over his laptop. He's squinting at the screen, deep in concentration. He's watching a video. It sounds like it's about alternate dimensions.

"Dad?"

"BAAAHH!" Dad jumps so hard, he stumbles off his chair and stands there, his hand clamped over his chest. "Blimey, Alex, you almost killed me!"

"Sorry," I say, scanning the room for his phone but not seeing it.

Dad chuckles. "Don't worry. I was just getting really into this. It's research for the book. Really interesting stuff. Hey, do you want to take a look at a couple of chapters?"

"Later," I say. "I was just stopping by and was wondering if I could use your toilet?"

"Of course!" says Dad, sitting back down. "But make sure you come and have a read afterwards, OK?"

I agree and turn back into the hall. The bathroom is next to the bedroom. Maybe his phone is still in there. I stick my head through the door. *Yes!* It's still on charge on his bedside table.

I sneak around the bed on my tiptoes and press the button on Dad's old phone. *Bingo.* One missed call and a voicemail from Peregrine Work. (Why has he put "work" on there? How many other Peregrines does he know?)

I hit the voicemail button and quickly delete the message. I'm about to leave, but I stop. If Peregrine doesn't get a response from Dad, he's going to call again. I need to think of a way to get something to him. Maybe a text?

I go to his contacts and find that Dad and Peregrine already have a chat log. It's mainly Peregrine telling him to be somewhere at a certain time and Dad just replying "OK".

"Hi Peregrine. Sorry I missed your call. That's fine re: Greenwood. Thanks, Carl."

I quickly hit send and put the phone back down.

"Alex?"

Dad stands in the doorway and this time it's me who jumps.

"You do know this isn't the bathroom, don't you?"

"Um, yes?"

"Good, because I was dreading to think you'd weed in my wardrobe," he says. "Everything all right?"

"Yeah," I say. "I was just seeing if you had a, um…" I scan the room for something until my eyes fall on a pile of books. "… *book* I couldn't find, but it looks like it must be at home after all."

"Must be," Dad chuckles. "Anyway, do you want to read a bit or not?"

I check my watch. I'm already late for Willow, and I've still got to go back to the depot. "Sorry," I say. "I've got to go."

Dad tuts sarcastically. "To see Willow, who's definitely not your girlfriend? Yeah, I get it. That's *two* other times you owe me, though, son."

I try and ignore the pinching feeling of guilt in the back of my head as I climb back on my bike and head back down the towpath.

The whole plan was so close to crashing down around me. I can't let that happen again.

The First Attempt

Carlos and Lloyd stood face to face in the time machine and stared at each other nervously as it slowly coughed and spluttered into action.

"You say you've used this thing before?" said Carlos.

"Sure," said Lloyd. "I went all the way back to prehistoric times. Lost the end of my finger in the jaws of a sabre-toothed tiger."

The juddering of the time machine grew more violent. Soon the small space began to fill with smoke.

"Don't worry about that," said Lloyd. "That's just, um, time smoke. It's safe to breathe."

But Carlos couldn't stand it any longer. He wrenched open the door and staggered out into the lab, wheezing.

Lloyd, after getting his breath back and wafting out the smoke with a towel, stood back and looked at his invention. "Just a few bugs that need working out, that's all. I'll have her right as rain by tomorrow."

Carlos's phone vibrated in his pocket. A

message from Alex. His heart leapt with excitement.

"Indie has volunteered to have her microchip. It's happening later today."

Carlos froze in horror. Then he desperately tried to call his daughter. It went straight to voicemail. He was on the other side of the country. There was nothing he could do.

"Lloyd," he said. "We need that thing to work. Now."

Chapter Twenty-Four

"You're an hour late!" Willow yells as I push the trolley up the hill. "What's going on?"

"Nightmare morning, I'm sorry," I puff.

"I was going to come down and look for you at the depot, but then I realized I don't actually know where this depot is, because you've never told me. I was about to give up and go home."

"Sorry," I say again, but this time there's an edge to my voice. "I've had enough stress to last me a lifetime this morning and I certainly don't need any more. If you had a phone, I could have let you know I was running late."

Willow throws up her hands like she's being held at gunpoint. "Well, I'm sorry, OK? Not all of us are rich enough to have phones and a set of plates we only use on special occasions."

A jolt of irritation passes through me. It's all right for me to make fun of Mum's fancy plates, but not Willow.

"What is wrong with you today?" I ask.

"What's wrong with me is you left me standing there like a melon."

I put the brakes on the trolley, open the lid and yank out her bag. "There you go," I say. "Better get started now as you're so keen to be done early."

Willow snatches up the bag and stomps away down the hill.

That was silly. It reminded me of Mum and Dad arguing. Just sniping over nothing.

Christmas Mick over the road wishes me season's greetings and I return it with a half-hearted wave.

All the way around my parcel run, I work up to apologizing to Willow. I shouldn't have snapped at her like that. Yes, she snapped at me first, but it doesn't matter. I just had a scary morning and I took it out on her.

When I get back, I find her waiting by the trolley, arms folded.

"Willow, I—"

"Just give me my next bag."

I do as she says. Maybe my apology can wait.

We repeat the same process for the next two bags and she still hasn't calmed down. Now is the time.

"What are you doing?" she says, as I stand there, not opening the trolley.

We're next to the cemetery gates, where I always chain the trolley up to the lamp post. Then, one of us goes up the road towards the pub, and one goes down towards the shop.

"Willow, I just wanted to say sorry."

"Wow, you're as late with your apology as you were arriving for work," she says, but it's with a hint of a smile.

"It's just been a horrible day and I—"

A car turns into the street by the pub and I think I recognize it.

I know I recognize it.

"I NEED TO TAKE YOU INTO THE CEMETERY!"

I grab Willow's hand and drag her through the gates.

"WHAT ARE YOU DOING?"

It's Peregrine's car, I know it. He's snooping

around, trying to find me. I drag Willow further into the cemetery and crouch behind a big headstone.

"Get down!" I hiss.

Willow crouches in front of me, her face flushed scarlet. "There had better be a good reason for this."

I creep up and squint through a gap in the hedge. Peregrine's car has stopped by the trolley. I shoot back down.

"Of course there is!" I say, looking around. "See that grave opposite? That's my granddad."

Willow looks over, then back at me. "He died in 1899. How is that your granddad?"

Come on, brain. Think of something better than that.

"It's actually my great-great-granddad?"

Willow groans and stands up. "This is silly, I'm going."

Panicking, I grab her hand and yank her back down.

"Ow, that hurt!"

"I'm sorry," I say. "We just need to stay down here for a while."

I peer around the headstone. Peregrine is at the gate, looking in. I wouldn't mind a zombie apocalypse at this point, just as a distraction.

"We're going to have to move," I whisper. "But we need to keep low."

"Why?" asks Willow.

I frantically hold up my finger to my mouth, too scared to even shush.

"I don't want to alarm you," I mouth, "but a man is after me."

"What?" Willow whispers. "Who even are you, Alex?"

I hear Peregrine's footsteps growing closer. "I'll explain later, but first I need us to move."

Looking both ways, I crouch-run behind the row of graves. A couple of rows back there's a big one: tall and wide with a praying angel on top. Whoever's buried there must have been pretty rich. Well, thanks, whoever you were.

When we reach the end of the row, I turn around and see Peregrine slowly walking up the path, his hands clasped behind his back. OK, he's not looking. After three, I'm going to make a run for it. One … two … *three.*

Still crouched, I zip as quickly as I can behind the big gravestone, then stand up, straight as a pole. Willow does the same and we stand facing each other, only centimetres apart.

"Why is that little man after you?" she breathes.

"I can't say right now." I peek out and see that Peregrine is now standing still, looking around the cemetery. I duck away again and when I have another look, he's heading back to the gates. I wait until I hear the car pulling away before I allow myself to breathe again properly.

"OK, I think it's safe," I say.

When we get back to the trolley, there's a note attached, on official letterheaded paper.

Carl,

I attempted to carry out a safety spot check today but was unable to locate you. Will try again at a later date.

Peregrine

Safety spot checks? Get a life. I go to open the trolley, but there's a thump on my shoulder.

"Ow!"

Willow is glaring at me, jaw clenched, mouth puckered. "Time to come clean, Alex."

I gulp. "OK … well."

"And I don't want any more lies. All this 'my

Mum didn't want me doing this job', or whatever. There's a real reason you're being so secretive around everyone and I want to know what it is, right now!"

Willow is angrier than I've ever seen her. She's got reason to be too.

I scrunch my eyes shut, then tilt my head back. When I open them again, the sky is the colour of porridge. I'm just going to have to tell her, aren't I?

I bring my face back down and look at her. Then I chicken out and look at a tree over the road. And I tell her everything: about Dad's book, forging a letter and a website, pretending there's a scheme, telling Mum and Indie I'm going out for bike rides and how now Peregrine might be on to me. I tell her every detail.

Willow rubs her forehead. "So you're doing all this because you think it will get your parents back together?"

"Well, yes," I say. "It probably sounds silly."

"Maybe." She shrugs. "What I want to know is why you didn't tell me this earlier."

"I, um, I don't know, Willow," I say to the tree. "I suppose I just felt embarrassed."

"Not as embarrassed as me, Alex," she says. I

force myself to look at her. Her chin is pointed, wobbling a little. "You've been lying to me this entire time."

"I'm sorry," I say.

"*I'm not a joke*, Alex." Her voice wobbles. I knew she'd be angry when I told her, but I hadn't expected this.

"I don't think you're a joke."

"Doesn't matter what you *think*, it's how you treated me! You're all the same."

"What do you mean? *Who's* all the same?"

Willow whips off her shades and glares at me. Her blue eyes are swimming with tears. "You must think I'm really gullible, falling for it this whole time. You've probably been laughing at me!"

"Will you just stop?" I yell. "I haven't been laughing at you, and I don't think you're a joke! To begin with, I just didn't know you that well, and then when I did, I really liked you and I didn't want you to think I was daft, that's all."

Oh. I just told Willow I like her, didn't I? Came right out with it. Let it out of my head, where it's nice and controlled, and out into the real world.

Willow roughly wipes a tear from her cheek with her hand and shakes her head. "Sure, sure.

Likely story. Well, why should I believe you now?"

Looks like the "I really liked you" slipped under the radar. Good. I think. The real problem now is I don't have a reason why she should believe me. I really don't.

"What are you waiting for?" Willow jabs me in the ribs, which really hurts. "Are you going to answer me, or are you going to stand there trying to come up with more lies?"

I have never met anyone as infuriating as Willow, not even Indie.

"They're not lies!" I shout back. "I've been honest with you now. Told you everything! How about you do the same?"

Willow tilts her chin defiantly. "What do you mean?"

"That trip to that prison-looking place, how upset you were? How you won't talk about your family? It's all looking a bit weird."

Without another word, Willow spins on her heels and stomps away, up the road, back towards the canal.

I call after her, but she doesn't turn around.

Chapter Twenty-Five

It's ten past nine and Willow isn't here. I hadn't expected her to be, but I had hoped. I've still bought food with me, just in case, but I'm looking down the hill and she's not coming. Looks like I'm doing the round by myself.

Everyone asks where the young lady is as I make my way around. Brenda even gives me a couple of bags of crisps to give to Willow when I see her.

I decide to go down to the boat. The crisps will break the ice. Maybe I can suggest a game of Mystery Crisp. I get to the bridge and look down to see if Willow is out, sitting on one of her chairs or cross-legged on the roof playing with Madge. But she's not there.

The boat's not there.

Surely she hasn't gone. She can't have! What about all her mum's jobs?

I chain up the trolley and run down the ramp and on to the towpath. I check the area next to where *Lola* was moored for any clues, any signs. I don't know what I'm hoping to find. It's not like she'd have left me a letter. Or would she have? No. There's nothing there. No trace that anyone was ever here.

She can't have gone far. Those boats don't go that fast. I reason she must have gone the same way we went last week, towards that weird gated-off place in the middle of nowhere.

I run until my lungs ache, and I don't know whether the tears in my eyes are from the effort or the thought that I might never see Willow again. Around the bend, I see a boat moored up. It looks like it might be *Lola*. Maybe. The closer I get, the clearer the colours become: the cracked sign, the lazy cat sunbathing on the roof.

When I get to the boat, I find Willow sitting on the towpath. On the floor in front of her is her magnet fishing line spread out on a blue blanket, and next to it there's a metal cylinder about the size of a tube of Pringles. It's caked in rust and dirt, which Willow is delicately brushing away with a cloth.

"Oh," she says. "It's you."

"I thought you'd left!" I splutter.

Willow makes a scoffing sound. "I'm hardly going to abandon my mum here, am I? Why would I leave?"

I kneel opposite her as she continues to clean. "I don't know. I thought maybe because I upset you."

Willow laughs without smiling. "As if I'd uproot my whole life because of you. Don't flatter yourself, mate."

At least she's talking to me and not telling me to go away. That's got to be something.

"What's that?" I ask, nodding at the metal thing Willow is cleaning up. Underneath the main body of the thing there's a thinner tube, with sharp-looking strips attached to the sides.

"Don't know," she says. "But it looks old. And if it's old, it might be worth a bit of money. It's solid too. Try and pick it up."

I'm a bit weirded out by all the gunk, but I'll give it a go. I don't want to upset her again. I grab the thing and lift it, but it takes a lot of effort.

"Wow, that weighs a tonne."

"You should have seen me dragging it out of the canal," she says.

I wipe my hands on the blanket and watch as Willow carries on cleaning it.

"So what are you going to do with it?" I ask.

"You know old Brenda who lives by the bridge?" she asks. "She's an antiques expert."

"Really?"

"Yep. She knows everything about them. She told me."

That explains why her house is full of old stuff, I suppose. I watch Willow's hands carefully clean the mud off the thing, a look of deep concentration on her face.

"Willow," I say.

She looks up at me. "What?"

"I'm sorry."

Willow stares at me for a few seconds, then nods quickly. "Want to help me get this thing on the boat?"

We take a side of the blanket each and lift the metal object on board. Then Willow turns *Lola* on and steers her around, heading back to where she was originally moored.

When we arrive, Willow goes inside and pulls a

rusty tyre contraption from under her bed. Taking it out on to the towpath, she grunts as she pulls at one side. It squeals and grinds until it rises up to become a wheelbarrow.

"It's important to have the right gear, Alex," says Willow, in a fake teacher voice. "Right, let's get her loaded up."

We carefully place our newfound treasure in the wheelbarrow.

I know I still have a couple of bags of post to deliver, but I can help Willow take this thing to Brenda first.

I take the handles of the wheelbarrow and start pushing, and find that the wheelbarrow makes it a lot easier to transport. Once we get off the bumpy towpath and up the ramp to the bridge, it's even easier. But just when I think things are getting too easy…

"LOOK WHO IT IS!"

Holden and Greg step out of the shadows, blocking our way. I hadn't seen either of them in ages, but judging by Holden's red, peeling nose, he must have been on holiday for a couple of weeks. Why couldn't he stay there? Permanently?

"Who's the girl, Ally boy?" Holden asks, giggling.

"All right, babe?" Greg leers at Willow with a wink.

"Ew," says Willow.

"What's in the barrow?" asks Holden.

"What is it with you and wanting things that aren't yours?" I snap back.

"Ohhh, are these the two losers who threw your trolley into the canal?" Willow asks me.

"Who you calling a loser?" says Greg, in his broken elephant voice.

"Well, obviously you," says Willow, before turning to me. "Not very bright, are they?"

Holden jumps forward and grabs our prize out of the wheelbarrow. I go to get it back, but he yanks it away, nearly dropping it. "Feel this, Greg!" he says.

Greg grabs it in his meaty hands.

"Pretty heavy," he says.

"Give that back," Willow growls.

"Nah," says Greg.

"You were warned," says Willow, and she launches herself at him, aiming a kick at his shin, which connects with a thud.

"Ow, you little—"

But Holden snatches the metal tube out of his

hand and runs down the street with it. Willow chases him, and I go to do the same, but Greg grabs me from behind, trapping me in a bear hug. I try and shout for help, but all the air is being squeezed out of my lungs.

In the distance I hear a yell. I have to get to Willow. I lift my legs and kick Greg in the exact same spot she did.

"AAAARGH!"

I take off down the hill, to find Holden frozen to the spot. Brenda is standing in front of him, holding out her arms like Gandalf.

"Keep perfectly still, lad," she is saying to him.

"Why?" asks Holden, smirking.

"That's mine!" Willow cries.

"I'm sure it is, my love, but I wouldn't go grabbing it if I were you."

Brenda reaches into her pocket and pulls out a tiny black thing about the size of a cocktail sausage, then she pulls something out of the back until it becomes about ruler-length. She holds it up to her eye, pointing it directly at the thing in Holden's hands. She takes it away from her eye, folds it back up, puts it in her pocket and nods thoughtfully. Then, she turns to us.

"You three should probably step back a bit."

"Why?" Greg asks.

"Because the thing that young hooligan is holding is an unexploded World War Two bomb."

The Second Attempt

Carlos and Lloyd arrived in 2002 at Peregrine's school. They eventually found him in the art studio. Even though he was but a boy, he was instantly recognizable: those sharp features and small, piercing eyes. They watched him for a while through the glass of the classroom door, as he diligently worked at a pottery wheel.

"All right," said Lloyd, pulling a heavy metal pipe out of his jacket pocket. "It's clubbing time."

Carlos grabbed the club out of his hands. "We can't do that, Lloyd."

"Why not?" asked the old man, indignantly. "We've come back to stop him."

"I know, but there has to be a better way," said Carlos. Even though he hated President Peregrine, he couldn't harm him as a boy. It wouldn't be right.

"OK, well, let's hear your bright idea, Mr I Don't Want To Club a Child," huffed Lloyd.

Carlos watched as a teacher loomed behind young Peregrine. He was a big man, and his bulk was just about contained by an ugly green sweater and grey slacks.

"What is that supposed to be?" he boomed, jabbing at the still-wet creation on the wheel.

"It's a vase, sir," said Peregrine, in a trembling voice.

"It's a monstrosity!" the teacher yelled, plunging his hands into the clay and squashing it back into a ball. "Do it again."

The teacher stalked away, leaving Peregrine to start again with quaking hands. Without thinking about it, Carlos entered the classroom. The teacher had his back to him, washing his hands in the sink.

"Hey," Carlos whispered to young Peregrine.

The boy looked up at him, his eyes swimming with tears.

"Don't listen to him, OK?" said Carlos. "You're really good at that."

Peregrine sniffed noisily. "Seriously?"

Carlos nodded. "Yeah! You just need to

practise, that's all. Keep practising and you'll be brilliant!"

Peregrine looked down at the slick clay turning slowly in his hands. "You really think so?"

"Definitely," said Carlos.

"Hey!" the teacher said as he turned around. "What are you doing in my classroom?"

"Giving this kid a bit of encouragement," said Carlos. "Which is what you should be doing!"

"My job is to mould these young people into strong adults," the teacher growled. "Now stay out of it!"

"Listen up," said Carlos, "humiliating them is only going to turn them into terrible adults. Trust me. I know."

"What do you know?" said the teacher, scornfully.

"I know a lot, my friend," said Carlos, gesturing at the kids, all now wondering who this strange man in their classroom was. "You have to remember, this is an important time in a child's life. They're trying to work out what they're good at and what they'll become. And you play a critical role in that. You get to help shape them, to bring out the best in them! That's a huge responsibility! And if you're lucky, you'll get to watch them truly blossom and become something ten times better than yourself."

Carlos didn't know where that speech came from. All he knew for sure is that he wasn't talking about Peregrine any more.

The teacher seemed to process this information, his eyes darting around the room. Carlos thought that maybe his words had broken through. That the teacher would rethink his cruel methods. Then the teacher's face turned the same shade of purple as a bottle of paint on the shelf next to him and he screamed, "You don't know what you're talking about. Now get out of my classroom!"

"Fine!" said Carlos, holding up his hands. "I'm going. But before I do, I have one more thing to say."

"Oh yeah, what's that?"

Carlos scooped up a glob of clay from a wheel next to Peregrine. "MOULD THIS!" He launched it across the classroom, where it splatted right in the middle of the teacher's forehead.

All the kids in the class roared with excitement. They clearly had been dreaming of doing that for years.

Carlos looked down and winked at Peregrine. "Remember what I said, OK?" In that moment, the boy looked so much like his Alex that he had to look away.

Back in the time machine, heading for the present day, Lloyd was still grousing about not getting to club the boy.

"Trust me," said Carlos. "This will have worked."

Carl stopped typing for a second. He had been hunched over the laptop and his tears were splashing off the keys. As if on cue, the door to the granny flat opened and Sandra walked in.

"Ohhh, Carl, what's the matter?"

"Nothing," he sniffed. "Just a bit of hay fever, that's all."

"There's no shame in getting emotional, Carl," said Sandra. "Especially at such a tough time. Do you want to come with me to church later?"

"I'll bear that in mind," he said, climbing to his feet. "For now, I think I'll just go for a walk."

"But, Carl, that might make your hay fever worse!" she called after him.

Chapter Twenty-Six

Holden screams like a distressed pig as we back away.

I can't believe we put a bomb on a boat, then wheeled it into the village. I'm doing my best not to scream.

I remember my granddad telling me that Tammerstone had a few bombs dropped on it during the war, usually by mistake when they were aiming for bigger cities, and that there was always the chance there were unexploded ones still around. I just imagined them to be bigger.

"Calm down," says Brenda to Holden. "The last thing you should be doing is making any sudden moves."

"I WANT TO PUT IT DOWN!" he cries.

"Don't do that, my dear," says Brenda, holding up a hand. "If you do, there's a chance the bump will make it go off. Best to just stay perfectly still."

"I DON'T LIKE THIS!"

Next to me, Willow giggles. Look, I don't want Holden to blow up, but if this had to happen to anyone, I don't mind that it's him. Indie is always going on about something called karma. I'm beginning to think there might be something to it.

Brenda pulls out an ancient mobile phone and makes a call.

"We need bomb disposal!" she yells. "There's a boy here at the canal holding a device that's been dragged out of the water. Get them here quick, because it's heavy, and I don't know how much longer he's going to remain intact!"

"AAAAARGH!" Holden screams.

Greg stands behind us, hyperventilating. "I can't believe I touched a bomb!" he says.

"That'll teach you to take things that don't belong to you, numbskull," says Willow.

"When you said there was something big down there, I didn't think you meant *explosives*," I say.

Willow shakes her head. "Can't believe it. I really thought I'd made some money there."

I look back at Holden. A dark patch spreads across his grey jogging bottoms.

"Did he…" says Willow, "… did he just pee his pants?"

I nod. "It appears he did." A smile spreads across my face. He can never bully me again after this.

Two police cars screech down the road and, without a word, Willow puts her head down and disappears back down the ramp to the towpath.

I call after her, but she ignores me.

"What's going on?" I yell louder, but she's pulling up the ropes and jumping on the boat and she's starting it up. I run to catch up and jump on with her.

"Seriously?" I ask.

She pulls away and takes us down the canal, away from the police.

"Willow, you're going to have to tell me what's happening sooner or later," I say. "Remember the fuss you made about me not telling you the truth?"

She fixes me with a look for a second, then turns her attention back to the open water, moving the gear lever up to top speed, which still isn't very fast.

"Are you on the run from the police? Is that it?" I persist. "What did you do?"

Ridiculous scenarios flash through my mind like asteroids through space. *What if she is a serial killer after all?!*

"Just stop talking for a minute," Willow snaps. "I need time to think."

"But—"

"I said stop!"

We carry on along the canal, through the lock in record time, past the place we stopped when she took me to that gated-off house. We go by a pub with a garden full of people, kids playing in a park, dogs yipping.

"Where are we going?"

Willow slows down the boat and pulls it to the side of the canal. Then she moors up and leads me up a path very much like the one she took me to when we visited the weird place.

A sign on the way in says "Cooley Country Park". Ah. I've been here before. Granddad used to bring me and we'd let the dog off the lead.

We follow the path until it opens up to a wide field, with a big hill on one side. Willow heads for the path leading up the hill and I follow. There are a few dog walkers around and we look weird power walking compared to their leisurely strolling pace.

At the top of the hill there's an obelisk and a sign saying "Lest We Forget" on it, but Willow isn't interested in that. She's staring into the distance. I follow her gaze and see the flashing lights of police cars way in the distance. Fishwick looks like a model village from here.

"So come on," I say. "Tell me what's happening."

"I don't think you want to hear it," she says, but I insist that I do.

Willow's eyes slide over to me. The usual steel is gone, replaced by something else. Something more like weariness.

"Well, I'm going to be staying here until they're gone, so I might as well."

Chapter Twenty-Seven

I'm from a town called Norberth. There's nothing much that's special about it. It's the type of place people pass through on the way to somewhere better. Still, it was home.

I haven't always lived on a boat. I used to live in a house with my parents. It wasn't as nice as yours, just a small one in the middle of a long row on a hill. Mum worked in a supermarket and Dad … look, Dad is not a nice person, I've told you that already. His job is to go to people's houses who haven't paid their debts and take things away from them: cars, TVs, jewellery, sometimes the house itself.

At dinner time, we used to sit in the lounge, our plates balanced on our laps and Dad would tell us all about his day, all the things he took. He seemed to enjoy it. He didn't care who he hurt.

"They should have kept up to date with their payments, then there wouldn't be any problems," he'd say.

It made me want to throw up.

Mum and I couldn't do stuff other people could. Mum wasn't allowed to have friends. She could go to work, and that was it. And on the rare occasions we went to parties as a family, Dad would tell us both what to wear, how to have our hair, everything.

In those moments when Mum and I were alone, I'd cuddle up to her and ask why she let Dad treat us like that. Sometimes it would make her cry. She'd tell me, "He's a good man and he loves us," but I never understood it. If either of those things were true, he wouldn't have acted like that.

This went on for years and years until finally Mum had enough. I don't know what happened, whether it was a specific reason or whether it was building up for a long time, but she told Dad we were leaving. So we went and stayed in this poky room on the other side of town.

Then one day, he came and took me out of school. The teachers didn't question it because why would they? He's my dad. And he took me back to our house. He said he'd seen to it that he gets to keep me and that Mum will never see me. He had lawyer friends thanks to his job, and he'd lied and falsified things to make it look like my mum wasn't fit to look after me. I'd hear her come and try and see me, but he'd never let her. One time, she stood out on the street and shouted up at me:

"I'm going to get you back, Willow, sweetheart, I promise!"

But then Dad forced her to go away, saying he'd call the police if she didn't.

One day, she left a note outside, hidden under a plant pot. There was a sunflower growing in the pot – she'd bought it for me – and it was my job to water it every night. But when I found the note, it had been raining, and one of the only words I could make out was "Fishwick".

I tried to escape a few times, during school and at night, but he always caught me. I found out later that he'd put a tracker on my phone. That's why I haven't got one: I left it behind.

The problem with Dad is he likes to show off about his job. If he'd repossessed a really expensive car, he would take me to see it, almost as if he owned it himself. I don't know why he thought I'd be impressed by that. All he'd done was take something away from someone else. It's not like it takes skill or anything.

One day, he drove me down to this boatyard where he showed me a barge he'd repossessed: Lola. He was all puffed up, going on and on about how he'd never repossessed a boat before and he'd steered it away himself and blah, blah, blah. I wasn't really listening. I was too busy planning.

I had looked Fishwick up, of course, and I knew a canal ran through it.

The next day at school, I started my research. Dad has a lot of filters and blocks on the internet at home, so it was barely worth using, but at school I had free rein. At lunchtimes I would sit and watch YouTube videos about how barges work, the steering, controls, gears, mooring and all that. Then I watched stuff about magnet fishing. I managed to find a pretty decent set for cheap in a local shop. I worked out that the journey from home to Fishwick would take a few days, so I took as much food as I could and stashed it in a bag.

Then, one night, I waited for Dad to go to sleep and grabbed his big bunch of keys, the ones he took everywhere with him. I knew the keys for both the boatyard and the boat were on there. It was just a case of figuring out which ones they were.

I left the house at two a.m. It was cold, the bag weighed a tonne and Madge kept wriggling in my arms, but I didn't stop, not even for a second. A police car pulled over and asked where I was going, but I spun them a line about camping in a field and they bought it, so I was able to carry on.

I managed to get into the boatyard and on to the boat pretty quickly, and I pulled out of there in the pitch black, bumping against the side every time. I just kept going, following the map as the sun came up.

So yeah, I was lying to you about being on my own, but I didn't know if I could trust you not to tell. Now I know I can.

The thing is, I don't know whether Dad has called the police or not. I think he'd try to look for me himself. After all, if the police pick me up, who knows what I might tell them? But I don't want to take the risk that he might have called them. He's so clever, I'm scared he'll convince them to send me back home, and I can't go back there, Alex. I just can't.

So, yeah, that's why I went to that place. I heard

there is a facility for women like my mum just outside Fishwick and I figured maybe she's there. But I still don't know. I need to, though. I have to find her before Dad finds me.

After telling me all of this, Willow sits back and closes her eyes. A single tear streaks down her cheek. I reach into my pocket and pull out a pack of travel tissues I always keep with me. When Willow opens her eyes and sees it, she laughs a little.

"Travel tissues," she says. "Trust you, Alex. So thoughtful."

She takes one, dabs at her eyes, then leans close to me, so close I can smell the coconut scent of sunblock from her skin, and she kisses me on the cheek.

I don't know what to say. I can't speak. *Does that count as my first kiss? Maybe?* I can feel my brain entering overthinking stress mode when,

BOOOOOOOOOOOOOM!

The sound of an explosion echoes from the other side of the valley.

Chapter Twenty-Eight

After hurrying back to the original mooring point, Willow stays in the boat, while I go up to the main road to investigate.

Police have blocked off the entire street and people stand behind barricades, watching. I see Holden sitting in the back of an ambulance, covered in a big shiny sheet, shivering. Looks like he didn't get blown up after all. I'm relieved. Kind of.

I walk past a reporter talking into a microphone. "Bomb disposal experts carried out a controlled explosion on the device," he is saying.

Huh. Well, that explains the boom, then. The first thing that comes to mind is that I have to go back to the boat and reassure Willow that the thing she dragged out of the canal hasn't killed anyone. But then I catch a glimpse of a postal uniform. It's Miriam. And she's standing next to my trolley talking to someone. She's talking to…

Oh no.

"DAD!" I yell, weaving my way through the crowd as fast as I can. "DAD!"

"So who's doing my round, then?" I hear him asking Miriam, but I leap in front of him before she can answer.

"Hello, son. What's the matter?"

I spin around quickly and look at Miriam, who is watching me with a confused frown.

"I have to tell you something," I say.

"But I'm talking to Miriam!"

"Yeah, but it's urgent. Quick!"

Dad gives Miriam a shrug and follows me to the ramp that leads to the towpath.

"What's up?" he says.

What *is* up? Besides my plan almost going up in smoke yet again, of course.

"What are you doing down here?" I ask, hoping the question will buy me time.

"Well, I came out for a walk and ran into Christmas Mick. He told me something about an unexploded bomb, so I had to get down here to see it," says Dad. "Might be good inspiration for the book."

"Right," I say. "Of course."

I glance over to my trolley. Miriam is still watching us. I have to get him away.

"Come on," I say. "Let's go and see Willow."

Dad chuckles. "If it's to tell me she's not your girlfriend again, I believe you, OK?"

Willow comes out when I call, cradling Madge in her arms. She looks a little relieved when she sees it's just Dad.

"It's all right," I tell her. "The police blew it up. No one was hurt."

"Wait a second," says Dad. "What's going on?"

Ah, now *that's* what I brought him down here for.

"Hey, Willow," I say. "Why don't we tell Dad the story of how we found the bomb?"

Carl arrived back at the granny flat, energized and ready to write. How could he not be? What excitement right on his doorstep!

The Present

Carlos and Lloyd stepped off the time machine. The lab was the same as how they'd left it.

"Well, it looks like we haven't affected the present timeline too adversely," said Lloyd. "I worried about that after I went to Victorian times and Jack the Ripper sliced my finger off!"

Dad grabbed his phone and googled who the current president was. He whooped when he saw it was someone called Roger McGuffin. Then he googled Peregrine's full name and saw he was now a renowned potter.

"We did it, Lloyd!" he yelled, clapping the old man on the back. "I'd better call my kids."

Carlos dialled Alex first. He was always more likely to answer.

"Is your sister OK?" he asked.

"She's fine," said Alex. "Just getting ready to have her microchip fitted."

"What?!" Carlos cried.

"Yeah, President McGuffin's microchip!" said Alex. "Surely you've heard of it? It's going to make our lives so much better!"

Lloyd gestured wildly at his computer screen.

It was a close-up of President McGuffin. He looked familiar. Carlos stepped closer and squinted at it.

Wait a second…

"It's the art teacher!" Lloyd groaned.

Carlos ran a hand down his face. Back to square one.

Carl chuckled to himself. What a twist! Readers were going to love that. They'd never see it coming! If he was totally honest, neither had he.

With the thrill of the completed chapter fading, Carl was able to think about what had just happened by the canal. Alex had been acting really strangely back there, dragging him away from Miriam like that. In fact, he'd seemed a bit … *off* … for the past few weeks. Carl had initially put it down to the stress of their separation, but there must be more to it than that. But what?

His mind buzzed with possibilities. What was Alex up to? Carl had barely seen him for weeks, and when he did, Alex was always in a rush to be somewhere. It was clear Alex was keen to get Carl writing again. Was it because Alex thought it would bring the family back together?

Carl's heart swelled with love. He remembered the first time he'd held each of his children. In both cases, he'd promised them silently that he wouldn't let any harm come to them, that they would be his world, his entire reason for living. Somewhere along the way, he seemed to have forgotten that promise. He had to put that right.

That night, Carl couldn't drift off; his mind was too frantic, thinking through his options. At half past two, he gave up trying to sleep and got out of bed, brewed a pot of coffee and sat in his usual writing chair. He'd found that writing this book had focused his mind, and helped him discover things about his own life.

Time to continue the story.

Carlos couldn't sleep that night. Lloyd's couch was lumpier than a sack of rocks anyway, but that wasn't the real reason for his unrest. It seemed like nothing they could do in that time machine would make a difference. It was almost as if these terrible technological advances were fate decided, and no rearranging of the presidents would do a thing to change that.

Carlos found himself wandering into the

brightness of the lab, blinking in the harsh light. The time machine was calling to him like a siren.

If he couldn't save the present, at least he could return to the past.

He stepped inside and set the coordinates for two years ago, to the time before his deep sadness had set in and he had wrecked his marriage. When life had been perfect and he hadn't even known it.

He pushed the big red button and closed his eyes as the machine slowly started up. Here we go.

Carl paced around the garden after finishing that chapter, the first rays of the sun appearing over the vibrant greens of Pete and Sandra's garden. He was full of nervous energy, unable to keep still.

The way he saw it, writing was his subconscious trying to communicate with him, telling him what to do. While he didn't have a time machine, he could create something nearly as good.

Ignoring Sandra staring at him from her bedroom window, Carl returned to the granny flat and began his preparations.

Chapter Twenty-Nine

I used to hate Sundays. Sure, it's a day of freedom, but it's also a day of dread. Your every move is haunted by the looming feeling of a yet another new week at school. Now, though, I'm just grateful for the rest. Only one more week of work to go.

I woke up this morning feeling recharged. Willow and I haven't made plans for today, and I'm thinking maybe it's best to leave her alone. Then again, she did tell me her big secret yesterday…

I can't stop picturing her all alone down there. I've thought about telling Mum, but then she'd get the police involved, and Willow doesn't want that. Plus, she trusts me. I can't let her down.

I take my phone off charge as I lie in bed and search her mum's name again. There has to be *some* sign of her somewhere. I do find women with the same name, but none of them are from Norberth, and many of them have photos with kids who aren't Willow.

I can hear music coming from outside. It's loud and annoying. And old too. Why is it getting louder? Sometimes people blast music out of their car windows, but this isn't moving. In fact, it sounds like it's in our front garden!

I go over to my window to see Dad standing there, holding a big portable stereo above his head that looks like it belongs in a museum. I open the window and lean out.

"DAD! WHAT ARE YOU DOING?"

He shouts something back at me, but I can't hear him because of the ear-bangingly loud music.

"WHAT?"

He pauses it and lowers the stereo so he's holding it under one arm.

"Is your mum there?" he asks.

"She's in the shower," I say.

Dad rolls his eyes. "Typical. I'm going to have to start the song over again now."

Mum comes into my room, one towel wrapped around her body and one on her head in a turban. Gently moving me aside, she steps in front of the window. I keep watching, terrified about what is about to happen.

"Carl?"

Dad stops fiddling with the stereo and looks up. "Oh, hello, Kate. I'm sorry about this. I had our song all queued up, and now I can't remember what number it was."

"*Carl*," Mum says.

"Now hold on a sec, let me just try this." Dad presses a button and a rap song with loads of swear words starts playing. He frantically jabs at the buttons, but he just ends up making it louder. He puts the stereo down on the floor and slaps at it until it stops.

"Carl!" Mum interjects again.

"I'm sorry, love," says Dad, looking up at her. "I was supposed to play the song we had as our first dance at our wedding. You know the one." He clears his throat and starts singing, "*Oooooh, I love you with all my heeeart and soouuul...*"

"Dad, oh my God, will you stop? The entire street can hear you."

I crane my neck and see Indie leaning out of the bathroom window.

"I don't care if the whole town hears me," says

Dad, spreading his arms wide. "Because I want them all to know how much I love my wife and how much I love my family!"

"Please, Carl," says Mum, rubbing her forehead.

"I witnessed a bomb going off yesterday, Kate," Dad goes on, ignoring Mum. "And it put things into perspective for me. Life is too short not to tell those you love what they mean to you."

"Then do it over text like a normal person!" Indie moans.

"And seeing our Alex with his young lady friend reminds me of us," Dad goes on. "We were young when we met. Barely more than kids ourselves, remember? Why can't we go back to that, eh?"

"Carl, I can't do this, not here," Mum says.

I close my eyes. How did this all go so wrong? Mum was *supposed* to see how much Dad has changed over the summer. And he *does* look better, happier, more rested, more *complete*, somehow. But for some reason that's still not enough, and he just looks like … a goober. And he's doing it because of me, because I've given him the chance to work on his dream, to become the person he wanted to be. But that person's clearly *not* what Mum wants any more. I feel sick.

"Then let me in and we can talk about it, OK?" says Dad. "Just hear me out one last time."

Over the road, I see people in nearly every house watching from their windows.

"For crying out loud, Mum, do as he asks before I die of cringe," says Indie.

Ten minutes later, Indie and I are sitting in the garden at the table while Mum and Dad talk in the lounge. We can see them through the patio door.

"How do you think it's going?" I ask.

Dad is currently sitting hunched forward with his head in his hands, so it was a silly question, really.

"How do *you* think it's going?" she asks.

I sit back and look at the sky. "This wasn't how it was supposed to go," I whisper.

"How *what* was supposed to go, Alex?" says Indie. "Your little secret post round?"

My head snaps down so fast it makes a whoosh sound. "W-what?"

"I figured it out a few days ago," Indie says, folding her arms, all smug.

I want to ask how, but at the same time, I don't want to admit to anything.

"As you know, baby brother, you've been

suspicious all summer, especially with your disappearing early every morning, Dad not being at work … well, I started to formulate a theory."

"All right, Sherlock, get to the point," I say.

Indie leans her elbows on the table and steeples her fingers. "I knew I could just follow you at any time, but I have my own life to live, Alex. And then *Willow* got involved, and food started going missing, which muddied the waters a little. I thought, *maybe there's something else.* But then the other day I was going out with my friend Fleur – you know, the one with a pony?"

"Get on with it," I groan.

"And I saw you, just pushing a big red trolley around, in broad daylight," she says. "I even took a picture. Do you want to see it?"

"No," I say, my head in my hands. "Have you told Mum?"

Indie leans over and pulls my hands away. "I may be many things, Alex, but a snitch isn't one of them."

I'm grateful for that, at least.

"I just want to know what you thought this was going to achieve," she says, her voice softer now.

I look back at Mum and Dad. Nothing much has

changed in their body language. "I thought Dad having time to write would change him. Turn him back into the old Dad."

"Yeah," says Indie. "And you've done that. But did you think it would make Mum forget everything and take him back? The world doesn't work like that, Alex."

"How would you know?" I snap at her, sick of being patronized. "Who made you a marriage expert?"

The back door opens and Dad trudges out, holding his stereo. He looks at us, gives us a thin smile, nods and heads around the side gate. I don't want to see Indie's "told you so" smug look, so I get up and follow Dad.

"So, how did it go?" I ask him.

Dad sighs deeply. "Not good, son. Not good."

"But why?" I ask.

Dad blinks. His eyes are watery and I quickly look away. I don't want to see him cry.

"It's complicated."

We walk on in silence for a while. I can see neighbours still looking at us from their windows. This must be the most entertainment they've had in ages.

"You're going to carry on writing, though, aren't you?" I say. "I mean, imagine if you get your book published! Mum's going to be so impressed."

Dad shakes his head sadly. "I don't know, son. I'm back to work next week. I think I'll probably knock it on the head."

I stop dead. "What?"

Dad stops and looks at me. "I gave it a go, but it probably won't work out. Best to just leave it."

Anger floods my body, beating at my defences like a raging storm against a sea wall. "Do you have any idea what I've done this summer so you could write that book?"

Dad shifts from foot to foot awkwardly. "I know you got me on that scheme, son, and I'm so grateful you did. But you shouldn't have put your faith in me. I'm nothing but an old let-down. And it's not only that, I'm trying to write about a family, and it's like our family and … and it's painful, Alex."

"Listen to me," I hiss, not really listening to him. "You are going to finish that book!"

"Whoa, steady on!"

"No, I won't steady on! If you knew what I'd been through, I…"

"What do you mean?" asks Dad. "What have you been through?"

My mouth opens. I'm going to tell him.

But I can't. Not now.

I shake my head, turn and head back home.

Chapter Thirty

I almost don't turn up for work. If Dad can't be bothered, then why should I? The only thing that gets me out the door is Willow.

When I chain my bike up outside the depot, something feels off. The radio isn't playing. This must be the first morning I've been here when it hasn't been on. Maybe it's broken. I push the door open and Lloyd and Miriam are both sitting on stools, facing another empty stool. They look at me as I enter with hooded, serious expressions.

No jokes from Lloyd, no "What time do you call this?" from Miriam.

"Um, hello," I say.

"Have a seat, son," says Lloyd.

"Am I in trouble?" I ask.

"Just have a seat," Lloyd says again. "We need to have a chat. Miriam?" He nods at the door and Miriam gets up, locks it and sits down again. I take my seat, which creaks as I ease myself on to it.

Lloyd leans forward. "This is an off-the-record meeting, son. What is said in here stays in here. No need for management to get involved."

Try not to panic, Alex. This could be about anything. You shouldn't always assume the worst.

"OK," I say, very much panicking. "So what's it about?"

Miriam and Lloyd share a quick side glance.

Miriam says, "We know there's no scheme, Alex."

My heart plummets. It's happening. I'm done.

"I looked into it," she says. "There never has been a scheme like this."

"Now, like I say," says Lloyd, holding up his four-and-a-half-fingered hand. "This doesn't leave these four walls. All we want to know is *what's going on.*"

There's no use trying to deny it. And I'm so tired, I can't come up with lies and excuses any more. So I just tell them. Tell them everything. When I'm finally finished, Miriam gets up and gives me a hug.

"You're a good lad, Alex," she says.

"Your heart's definitely in the right place," Lloyd agrees. "I might not understand your methods, but I admire your determination."

Miriam sits back down and sighs. "I knew Carl was struggling, we both did. Then when I saw him after that bomb situation the other day, he looked great, like a different man. Completely refreshed."

"And you're saying this is the last week you'll be doing it?" asks Lloyd.

I nod.

Lloyd and Miriam look at each other for a long time. "Peregrine's been sniffing around," says Lloyd. "If he catches you … we had no idea. Do you understand?"

I nod again.

Lloyd smiles a little. "I hear there's a girl with you as well."

"Yeah," I say, and I catch myself smiling a little, thinking about her.

"And why is she involved?" Miriam asks.

"She's trying to find her mum," I say, carefully. "She thinks her mum's moved to Fishwick."

Lloyd scratches the back of his ear. "What's her mum's name?"

"Eve Haunton."

Lloyd lets out a long breath. "That rings a bell, you know."

"She took me to this place in the woods behind a huge gate, but they wouldn't tell her if she was in there," I say.

"That's the women's refuge," says Lloyd. "But she's not in there." He stands up and stares at his fitting, and I get up and join him. My heart is racing. Could this be it?

"Eve Haunton! I remember now. She's in the flat above Mrs O'Reilly at 72 Nightingale Avenue. It was empty for months, then she moved in."

"Are you sure about that?" I ask.

He nods. "Positive. When you've been on a round as long as I have, you notice new faces and remember names. She's there, all right."

I make a note of the address.

"OK," says Lloyd. "Enough of this faffing about. Let's get on with the job, shall we?"

The Last Letter

Something went wrong. The time machine reached its destination two years before, and the door opened, but Carlos couldn't leave. An invisible force kept him rooted to the spot. His wife and children were sitting together at the kitchen table, but they didn't know he was there too. He reached out for them, screamed their names, but he was like a ghost.

Then the door slammed shut and the machine shook violently. In a second, he was back in the present day. Lloyd furiously grabbed Carlos by the shoulders and launched him out on to the hard lab floor.

"What do you think you're doing, Carlos?"

Carlos blinked back tears as he scrambled to his feet. "I wanted to go back, to be with my family," he said.

Lloyd growled under his breath. "You know what I've realized, Carlos? I've realized that I've wasted so much time trying to go back. And it was pointless. I should have lived in the now, tried to make that better. Living in the past is a fool's errand."

Carlos took a jerky breath. "What do you mean?"

Lloyd softened his stance and gripped Carlos's arm. "When you constantly look to the past, you can miss things that are happening right under your nose. You understood what Peregrine needed, and yeah, it looks like you fixed things for him. You've got a talent for that kind of thing. But, like a fool, you drew the wrong lesson from that experience. It's not about going back to the past – time travel isn't what's important here; it's not what will save us all. It's not the change you need to make." He dropped his hand from Carlos's arm. "Go home. See your boy."

"My boy?" Carlos thought about Alex, about the strange ways he had been acting. A thought was beginning to form in his mind, and the more he worked on it, kneaded and worried it like a damp lump of clay on a potter's wheel, the clearer it became.

Thanking Lloyd, Carlos left his house and caught the next bus back home.

Chapter Thirty-One

I rushed out of the office with my trolley and chained it up on the hill. I'm about half an hour ahead of my usual time, so Willow isn't here yet. I'm so excited for her. I keep picturing how she'll react when I tell her. Will she want me to go with her? I will if she does, but I bet she'll want to be on her own. I think about heading straight down to the boat, but maybe I'll do the first bag as I'm early. Then, when Willow arrives as normal, I can just drop the news all casual. I think she'll appreciate it.

I pull my lightweight trolley out of the big one and am about to load it up with the bags when a car pulls up alongside me. It's an expensive-looking model, but covered in dirt. The tinted driver's side window rolls down and a man looks at me, smiling. He's about Dad's age, his head a big block framed by closely cropped ginger hair.

"Hi, mate," he says, in a smooth voice. "You a paper boy?"

I think about saying I'm actually a postal worker, but that would just seem weird, so I say, "Um, yes."

"Good." He grins. "You haven't seen a canal boat called *Lola* around these parts, have you?"

An icy chill blasts me all over. The man smiles but his eyes are dead.

"No," I say. "No, I haven't."

The man's smile doesn't drop. He just shrugs and says, "Never mind." Before I know it he's screeching away, up the hill.

I have to warn Willow. I run as fast as I can to the bridge. It's only when I get to the bridge that I notice I've been pushing the lightweight trolley the entire way. Why didn't I just leave it? Never mind. There's *Lola*, and I can't see the car around, so it looks like he hasn't found her. If I can get Willow out of the boat and to her mum's flat, she'll be safe.

"Alex, what are you doing here?" Willow asks me when I arrive, sweaty and panting outside the boat.

"We need to get out of here," I say.

"Well, I was about to do that anyway," she says. "What's going on?"

"Two things," I say, struggling to catch my breath. "I know where your mum is."

"What?" she gasps. She leans against the boat like she's about to faint.

"But on the way here, a man stopped and asked me if I'd seen this boat."

Willow's face changes from surprise to horror. "What did he look like?"

"Big," I say. "He was driving a dirty BMW."

Willow stands up straight and nods. "We need to get to my mum right now."

We turn and head to the ramp, but our way is blocked by a bulky shadowed figure.

"Hello, sweetheart," the shadow says, grinning with dead eyes.

Carl closed the laptop and stared at the flowery wallpaper. The impact of his realizations reverberated around his head as though a massive bell had been struck in the centre of his skull.

He had been living in the past for so long. Ever since that school reunion he'd been pining for a time that could never be recreated. It stopped him from seeing what was really happening. He and Kate had been growing apart for years, each headed in their own direction. It was no one's fault, it just happened without either of them necessarily realizing it.

Things change. Nothing stays the same. And that's not always a bad thing. Just look at Alex. To Carl, he was still his baby boy, but look at what he had done! At least, what Carl thought Alex must have been doing. He needed confirmation.

Chapter Thirty-Two

Willow tries to run, but her dad grabs her by the back of the neck.

"Let go of her!" I say, but he ignores me.

"Do you have any idea how much money you've cost me, stealing this boat?" he growls.

"That's all you have to say?" spits Willow. "You weren't worried about me? You weren't scared for my safety? All you cared about was *the boat*?"

"You need to watch your mouth," he warns, his voice full of darkness.

"Let go of me!" Willow demands.

"We are getting on this boat and we're taking it back to the yard," he says, bundling her past me, down the path.

"I'll call the police!" I yell, pathetically.

"And say what? That I'm taking my runaway daughter home and returning a stolen boat? Good luck with that, boy." Then he stops and looks at me over his shoulder, still gripping Willow's neck. "And thanks for leading me to her. I could tell you were lying from your face."

I feel sick all over again. This too is my fault.

Willow kicks and claws and scratches, but her dad is too strong. In my desperation, I launch the trolley at him, but it bounces off his back like it's nothing and clatters on to the floor of the boat. He throws her inside, pulls up the ropes and steps on behind her. In seconds, they're away.

I can't let this happen. I have to do something. But what?

My legs are already moving, like I'm in a computer game being controlled by someone who thinks that if I die, I'll just respawn.

I pick up speed and jump on to the back of the boat, crouching behind next to the back doors that had slammed behind them.

I peer between the closed doors. Willow is sitting at the table with Madge. Willow's crying, but she looks angry. If I can get her to come towards me, we can jump off and escape. I turn the latch and open the door a crack.

"Willow!" I whisper.

She looks up and sees me. "Alex, what are you doing?" she hisses.

"Just come this way," I say. "We can jump off!"

She shakes her head. "He'll find me, you know he will."

"We can get to your mum's before he realizes," I say. "Come on!"

Willow's face twists, then I see her jaw clench as she makes the decision.

She grabs Madge and runs over to me; we crouch on the little ledge. The boat is going top speed now, and the towpath is further away than I thought. We might end up in the water, but it will be worth it.

"Are you ready?" I ask.

"Yeah," says Willow.

"Here we go—"

SMASH!

The shutter flies open and Willow's dad grabs both of us, dragging us inside. We both struggle, but he's too big and strong. He throws us down and locks the doors at the back.

"Who are you anyway?" he seethes, pointing at

me, his fingers the shape of a pistol.

"He's my friend," says Willow.

"We'll see about that," says her dad. "I told you, no talking to boys."

"You told me a lot of things," says Willow. "But I'm not listening any more."

"Watch your mouth, young lady," he warns. "That's no way to talk to your father."

I see it now, what Willow was talking about. That darkness, that power.

"But you're not a dad," says Willow. She nods her head at me. "*His* dad is a real dad. You're nothing but a bully."

"His dad, huh?" he says, his eyes appraising me. He looms over me and holds out his hand. "Give me your phone."

I don't want to, but I realize I don't know what he'll do if I say no, so I hand it over.

He turns and stomps to the front of the boat. The engine dies. I hear him jump off the boat and moor up. I think maybe we could run, but he'd catch us. There's no one on the towpath – no joggers, no dog walkers, no one. He re-emerges and orders us off the boat.

"Where are we going?" asks Willow.

"Somewhere I can keep an eye on you until you calm down," he says. "Somewhere you can learn some *respect*." He stares at me with icy eyes. "You're coming too, boy."

Carl's car screeched to a halt next to Lloyd and Miriam's van. They had pulled up for their mid-morning cup of tea just like they always did at the same time every day. When they saw him get out, their faces took on a strained, unsure look. Lloyd wound down his window.

"Carl!" said Lloyd, his voice wobbling a little. "Long time no see."

Carl shifted uneasily. "Yeah, it's been a while. Hey, I've got a question for you. It's going to sound a bit weird."

Lloyd and Miriam shared a quick look. "Sure," says Lloyd.

Carl gripped the bottom of the van window. "You know how I've been off for a few weeks? Well, who has been my replacement?"

Neither Lloyd nor Miriam knew what to say. They had promised to keep Alex's secret but hadn't considered that it might be from his own dad.

Carl took a breath. He knew he could be about

to make himself look ludicrous, and the last thing he needed to do was give these two ammunition to mock him. They had enough already.

"Is it … is it Alex?"

Lloyd turned away from Carl and looked at Miriam. He knew *he* couldn't do it, but maybe she could?

"He told us there was a scheme, Carl," she said. "He was really convincing."

Carl nodded and headed back to his car. Part of him was angry that Alex had lied for so long. But he mainly felt … *pride.* His boy had done all this, sacrificed his whole summer, to let his dad chase a dream. To try and put the family back together.

Just the thought of it made tears prickle Carl's eyes. He had to go and find him.

Carl turned the car around and headed up the hill. That was where the round started, so Alex couldn't be far off. Carl saw the trolley chained up at the top. How had Alex done it every day? How had he had the strength?

Carl got out of the car and looked up and down the hill. There was no sign of Alex. He considered the possibility that maybe Alex had seen him and was hiding. How many other close calls had there been? His mind flashed back to the night at the pub, how nervous Alex had been. It all made sense now.

"Carl! Merry Christmas!"

Carl shielded his eyes from the sun and saw Christmas Mick waving at him from his drive, the red nose on his Rudolph jumper blinking rhythmically.

"Merry Christmas, Mick," he replied, just like he always did.

"That boy's been doing a terrific job in your absence," he said. "Like a hardworking elf, he is."

Carl headed over the road to get closer to the eccentric old man. "Say, Mick, you don't know where he is, do you?"

Christmas Mick shook his head, his antlers wobbling. "I saw him earlier, though," he said. "He talked to a fellow in an old BMW. Then when the car left, Alex took off that way." He pointed over the hill towards the canal bridge. "It was ever so strange. He looked quite panicked."

Carl thanked Mick and got back in the car. A sour sickness spread through his stomach. Something wasn't right. Something wasn't right at all.

Chapter Thirty-Three

Willow's dad grips the backs of both our necks and forces us up a path through some trees. He takes us all the way to the main road and through a gate. I hope for a car or some kind of passer-by, but it's still deserted.

The old barn sits alone in the middle of an overgrown field, with corn stalks over our heads. A big chunk of the roof has fallen in. He's taking us there, I know it.

Willow and I look at each other. I can tell we're thinking the same thing. We could try and make a run for it. If we split up, at least one of us could escape. Then they could send for help.

"Three," I mouth at Willow.

"Two," she mouths back.

"One," we both whisper.

I make a break for it.

"Ugggghh."

The grip on my neck tightens and I'm choking.

"You two must think I was born yesterday," Willow's dad says and chuckles. He kicks the barn door opens and shoves us inside. I hear things scurry away in the darkness. The only light comes from the hole in the roof and it illuminates half of Willow's dad's face.

"All right, kids," he says, rubbing his rough hands together. "We are going to stay here until the two of you have learned some manners."

Carl screeched the car to a halt on the canal bridge and looked for any sign of Alex. He didn't know what he thought he'd find, but there was nothing.

"Hey up, Carl!" Brenda hobbled down the drive, with a black bin bag. "You back on the job?"

"Not exactly, Brenda!" said Carl, trying to keep his voice even. "You haven't seen the post boy around, have you?"

Brenda smiled. "He's been doing a wonderful job, Carl."

"Have you seen him this morning?"

"Come to think of it, yes," said Brenda. "I happened to look out of the window earlier on and I saw him run down the towpath with his little trolley. I thought perhaps he'd been caught short and wanted to use the facilities on that young girl's boat."

Brenda's theory calmed Carl a little. It made sense. Alex had always been squeamish about the toilet in the depot, so maybe he just wanted to use Willow's. But when Carl turned and looked down at the towpath, the sick feeling in his stomach only intensified. The boat was gone.

Carl ran down the ramp on to the towpath. He stood for a second, staring at the spot where the boat had been parked before and tried to remember which way the barge faced. Surely, that would be the way they went.

"Oh, there he is!"

Carl looked around for the voice. It took him a while to see Mr Greenwood up a tree in his garden, trimming back the branches.

"Finally decided to show your face after sending children to do your work for you, have you?"

Carl jabbed a finger at Greenwood, finally able to talk to him in kind now that he wasn't in uniform. "I am not in the mood. Have you seen my son?"

Greenwood chuckled. "Yes I have. I've seen him all summer, blatantly breaking the law. I complained to your employer, but do you think they listened? Waste of time, the lot of them."

"Now you listen to me, you miserable old man," Carl growled. "Have you seen him or not?"

Greenwood was so shocked he almost dropped his shears. "Well, that is an unacceptable way to speak to a customer."

"I'm not at work, Greenwood. Now answer my question."

Mr Greenwood was rattled by this. He wasn't used to a postman talking back to him to his face. "Well, actually, yes I have, as it happens."

"And where was he?"

Greenwood pointed down at the towpath with his blade. "I saw him running after a boat. This rough-looking fellow was steering it."

"Rough-looking fellow?" asked Carl, his mind awhirl. "Did you recognize him from anywhere?"

Greenwood shook his head. "Never seen him around here before. I reasoned he's probably someone else your son and that girl have wronged. Wouldn't surprise me."

"Which way did they go?" Carl cut in, balling his hands into fists.

"Up there," said Greenwood, pointing the way. "About half an hour ago."

Carl didn't need to hear any more. He was off.

"Let us go!" says Willow.

"And why would I do a thing like that?" asks her dad, pacing along the thin shafts of light spilling through the cracks in the wooden shell of the barn.

"Because kidnapping is illegal?" Willow spits.

He forces us to sit on the cold, muddy ground, backs to a grimy trough.

Through the darkness, a laugh echoes. "Where did you get this attitude from, my dear? Because you certainly didn't have it when you were at home." He steps closer to us, a light beam illuminating half of his face. "But we'll make sure it's gone by the time I get you back there." His cold stare switches to me. "What have you been saying to her, boy?"

I don't know how to respond to this man. I can't cope with this. It's about as far from the Natural Order of Things as you can get.

"I … I haven't been saying anything," I say, floundering. "I've been helping her."

This doesn't stop the stare. His mouth tightens into a snarl. "You've been helping her run away from me."

"No, I—"

A hand grips my face under my chin. I can't move my mouth. The fingers dig in. It hurts.

"Let go of him!" I feel Willow slapping at him, but he bats her away with his other arm like she's nothing.

"I run a tight ship," he hisses. "I don't ever let boys hang around my family. So when some boy slithers his way in and tries to take one of them away, I don't take kindly to it. Just ask that man who was 'just a friend' of my wife's. He wasn't such a friend after that."

His fingers dig in harder, pushing in on my teeth. I groan in pain.

"I said, *let go of him!*" Willow screams.

"Oh, I will," he growls. "As soon as I've taught him a lesson."

Chapter Thirty-Four

I know they call those trolleys lightweight, but when they're smashed across a person's head, they must feel pretty heavy.

Dad stands over Willow's dad as he lies on the ground, unconscious.

"Are you two OK?"

I jump up, run over and hug him. I can't remember the last time I hugged my dad, but I don't care. I'm just so happy to see him. He leads us outside, still holding the trolley in case Willow's dad gets back up.

"How did you find us?" I ask.

"I thought about what you said to me the other day. Things started adding up in my head and I put it all together. There's no scheme, is there?"

I shake my head.

"You were doing all this to try and sort us out, weren't you?"

I nod.

Dad sighs. "Oh, son." He nods at the shape of Willow's dad lying on the floor. "Who's that?"

"He calls himself my dad," says Willow. "But he's not."

Dad smiles at Willow kindly. "I'm going to have to call the police now, sweetheart."

Willow nods. "Good."

I reach for her hand and she squeezes mine. I say, "And then we'll get you to your mum, OK?"

Willow looks at me and smiles. "Yeah. Sounds good."

Chapter Thirty-Five

The police have just taken Willow's dad away. He's been arrested for kidnapping. They're going to have to take *Lola* too as it's stolen property. But it doesn't look like they're going to press charges against Willow. Not after she told them everything.

A police officer takes her to her mum's address, which I gave them, and I get Dad to follow in his car. There's a row of shops on Nightingale Avenue, and according to Lloyd, Willow's mum lives above one of them.

I see Brenda going in with her tartan shopping trolley.

The police car has pulled up and the officer lets Willow out, holding Madge. As soon as Dad parks up, I jump out too.

That's when I hear a cry coming from around the corner.

Willow hears it too because she turns to see a woman standing there, her hand clamped over her mouth. Willow runs over to her and jumps into her arms. They stand there, not speaking, eyes closed, just holding each other.

Dad comes up next to me and puts his arm around me, squeezing my shoulder. "Love you, son," he says.

"Love you too, Dad," I say. I don't think I've said that since I was about seven.

The commotion and the police presence have drawn a bit of a crowd – for Fishwick, that is, and to be fair it's the busy time of the week on the High Street. There's a lot of hugging and chatter going on, as Willow's mum has clearly made a lot of friends here and she wants to introduce Willow to all of them. I don't know how many minutes go by before a big car pulls up and Peregrine hops out, but there's nothing I can do. He's seen us.

"Ah ha!" he says, jabbing his finger at Dad. "I knew Mr Greenwood was telling the truth! You haven't been at work all summer and your son has been doing your job. Look, he's even wearing a red shirt!"

"You're imagining things," I say to him.

"I am not, my boy," Peregrine honks. "And you have been committing a criminal offence." He nods to the police officer who has been watching. "You should investigate."

"Got any proof of that, Peregrine?" asks Dad, folding his arms.

"All I need to do is ask the residents! They'll tell me," says Peregrine.

"Well, I'm a resident," says Brenda, "and you're talking a load of codswallop. Carl has been delivering my post the whole time. And a very fine job he's been doing too. There's another couple of residents here, I bet they'll back me up." As soon as she says it, Christmas Mick appears in his reindeer jumper and paper crown. Everyone is on our side, even if I lied to them.

"Oh yes," he says. "Carl has been here every day. Isn't that right, Mr Greenwood?"

Me and Dad look at each other. Even Willow, finally breaking away from her hug with her mum, is watching.

Mr Greenwood stands in the doorway of the shop, a bottle of milk dangling from his hand. He looks at Dad, then at me, then at Peregrine, in a triangle shape, again and again and again. Finally, he addresses Peregrine.

"I must have been mistaken, sir," he says. "Sorry about that."

And with that, he turns and leaves.

Maybe he's all right after all.

Peregrine stands there, his face turning purple. "I'll find someone who'll confirm it," he says. "You see if I don't."

Chapter Thirty-Six

HERO POSTMAN SAVES THE DAY

Drama came to the sleepy village of Fishwick yesterday when two children were forced aboard a canal boat and kidnapped. Fortunately, Carl Norris, father of one of the children, was able to track down the trio and take the assailant out with a blow from his postal trolley.

Carl, 42, declined to be interviewed, but local residents spoke glowingly about their postie.

"He's simply wonderful," said Brenda Glover, 82. "He's been my postman for twenty years and he's always friendly,

> polite and has time for everyone."
>
> Michael Kringle, 65, agrees. "This village wouldn't be the same without Carl. He's a big part of the community. Merry Christmas!"

I've kept all Dad's newspaper cuttings and saved all the online articles to my favourites. When I showed them to him, he teared up.

"I suppose I just didn't realize people cared that much," he said. "If I'd known that, I wouldn't have felt like such a waste of space."

It's been a week since we got kidnapped by Willow's dad. We've all been interviewed by police, and Willow and her mum have given statements, not only about what happened last week, but about everything that came before. For now, Willow has moved into the flat with her mum, and it looks like they might be staying.

I hope so. I really, really hope so.

While I was at Dad's, he gave me a copy of his book, *The Last Letter*, all printed out. He said it still needs some work before he starts sending it to agents, but I've read it and I love it. I blasted through it in a day. So much stuff makes sense now.

So that's why I waited until Indie had gone out and took it into the lounge to Mum.

She smiled at me when I walked in. She's gone pretty easy on me, considering I've been lying to her all summer. I guess being kidnapped does that.

"I've got something to show you," I said.

"Not another job application, is it?" she said, with a laugh.

"It's Dad's book."

Mum looked at me wearily. "Really?"

"I think you should read it," I said.

Mum muted the TV and folded her arms. "And what would that achieve, exactly?"

"I just think you'd see things differently." I placed it on the arm of the chair. "Just give it a chance."

"Alex, I—"

"Please, just have a quick read," I said. "I won't ask you to do anything else."

Mum flipped through the pages, then looked up at me. "Fine."

I checked in a few times last night to see if she'd finished it. She called it "pestering", but I don't think that's true. Anyway, she's just called me down to the living room, and when I walk in, she's sitting on the sofa with the book. She taps the cushion next to her.

"You've read it?" I say.

Mum nods, her face giving nothing away.

"It's brilliant, right?" I say. "I mean, he did that all by himself!"

Mum smiles tightly. "It is very good. But I always knew he could write."

I wait for her to say something else, but it doesn't look like she is going to. "Soooo," I say, elongating the word so much you could almost see a question mark float out of my mouth. "What happens now?"

Mum takes a deep breath and places her hand on my knee. "Did you read this properly, Alex?"

"Of course I did!" I say. "It was great. Microchips, time machines, battles. What more do you want?"

"It's the time machine aspect I wanted to talk about," says Mum. "I can see what your dad is saying with that, and he's right."

I furrow my brow and stare at the carpet. All I remember is him and Lloyd going back and whacking some clay at an art teacher.

"You can't go back to the past," Mum says, gently.

"I still don't know what you mean," I say, even

though I'm starting to. I just don't want to.

"I still love your dad, you know," she goes on. "I always will, in a way. But things have changed, and I don't see how they can go back."

I try and stop my eyes filling with tears, but it's no good. "I don't understand. If you love each other, why … why?" I can't finish the sentence because I don't know how to.

Mum squeezes my hand. "Neither do I, my son. And if pure effort was enough to put a marriage back together, well, you would have fixed it ten times over."

"So this has all been for nothing," I say, trying and failing to swallow the boulder in my throat.

"No, it hasn't," Mum says. "Look, your dad was lost for a long time. What you did" – she picks up the printed-off book – "is help him find himself again. And help him realize that he hasn't wasted his life."

I think about it for a second, and she's right. But I've still failed. I look at a framed photo of the four of us on the mantelpiece. We're on holiday somewhere, I can't remember where. We're by a sea wall: Mum, Dad and Indie are standing, and I'm sitting with my legs dangling. I'm probably about eight, and even though I can't remember where we are, what I can remember is how happy I felt.

"But how am I…?" I start, but my voice cracks and I can't catch my breath. I don't really know what I want to ask anyway.

Mum lets go of my hand and puts her arm around me. "Look," she says, "sometimes in my job, I have to show people around some real dumps. I'm talking no carpet, overgrown garden, ceilings falling in, collections of sinister dolls taking up an entire bedroom, you name it."

I want to ask what this has to do with anything, but my voice still hasn't recovered.

"And I have to look people in the eye and say, 'It might not look like much, but this house is solid. All it needs is a little care and attention and you can make this something special'." Mum strokes my hair, like she used to when I was little. "And it sounds like a line, something I'm just spouting because I want them to buy the house, but I mean it, I really do. And it's how I feel about life too."

I give her a "what do you mean?" look.

"Life might not be what you wanted or imagined," Mum goes on. "In fact, it might be horrible. But it always has a solid base and, with a bit of work, you can make it special. We all can."

I think about Dad, sitting in Uncle Pete's annexe, tapping away at his book.

I think about Indie, going off to uni soon.

I think about Willow, starting again with her mum.

I think about us, figuring out how we're going to work as a family.

There's no such thing as a Natural Order of Things any more. And maybe that's as it should be.

Chapter Thirty-Seven

ONE YEAR LATER

"How do I look?" I ask Willow as we walk down the steps to the pavement. "Is my dickie on straight?"

"Nope," she says, leaning in to adjust it.

"How about me?" she asks, suddenly stopping and standing back. She's wearing a long red dress that matches her hair, which is done up in a beehive with two curled strands cascading down each side of her face.

"Eh," I say, with a shrug.

I dodge the arm punch I know is coming, but she's too quick and catches me anyway. She always does.

We continue walking and turn the corner from

Willow's new house where she lives with her mum, on to the High Street, where the lamp posts by the depot are strung up with fairy lights.

THE LAST LETTER BOOK
LAUNCH THIS WAY.

Dad, Lloyd and Miriam have done a great job making the depot look nice. They cleaned, painted and even ripped up the disgusting old rug. I was there when they did that. Lloyd saluted after he threw it in the skip and said, "So long, old friend."

There are vines stuck to the walls and various surfaces, and fake flame torches add to the atmosphere. The stereo is on, but rather than the same old radio station, there's twangy guitar music that sounds like it's from the desert.

After Dad became a bit of a celebrity hero, some publishers were interested in reading his book and one of them actually wanted to publish it. He hasn't made tonnes of money from it – he's still a postman – but the main thing is, he's happy. He goes to work, dreams up ideas while posting letters, then goes home and writes them. It's a pretty good life.

Dad greets Willow and I as we walk in. He's

wearing a smart new purple suit. Lloyd and Miriam are here ready to hand out drinks and snacks too. Lloyd has said he can't wait to thrill these fancy book folk with all the tales of how he lost the end of his finger. "They'll all be begging me to write my autobiography," he kept saying.

Soon, people start to file into the small space. There are staff from the publisher, someone from the local paper, but mainly it's people from Fishwick. Brenda comes in wearing a green tweed suit and hat. Christmas Mick arrives soon afterwards with tinsel, mistletoe and mince pies. They know I'm Carl's son now but would never tell Peregrine I was delivering. Uncle Pete and Auntie Sharon are there, of course. Mr Greenwood even shows up with an envelope for Dad and a strong handshake.

The room soon fills up and spills out into the car park. I catch a glimpse of Peregrine, who long ago gave up trying to prove I was doing Dad's round, enjoying the festivities. Dad had to change his name in the book, so it's now President Peterson rather than President Peregrine, but it's still pretty obvious to everyone except him who it's based on.

"This is special, isn't it?" says Willow, taking a sip from her mocktail.

"Yeah," I agree.

"I mean, look, your dad has achieved his dream, and he's surrounded by people who love him, and it's all thanks to you," she says.

"It's not all thanks to me," I say, feeling a flush of pleasure at a rare non-sarcastic compliment from Willow. "Dad wrote it."

"Yeah, but he wouldn't have done it if you hadn't made him," she says. "You should be proud!"

Mum, Willow's mum and Indie make their way towards us through the crowd. Our mums have become good friends over the past year, especially after my mum got her mum a job in her office. Indie has been at uni since last September, but has come back tonight especially for Dad's book launch. She's been telling all her professors that her dad is a published author, but I don't think it's helped her get better grades.

"Little broooo!" she says, grabbing me in a headlock. "It's so nice to see you, squirt. He's not been driving you up the wall has he, Willow?"

"Hmm, a little bit," she replied.

"What happened to your voice, anyway?" I ask, wriggling free and flattening my hair.

"Nothing," says Indie. "What are you even talking about?"

"You've gone *posh*," I say.

"Oh shut uuuup," she says, all posh-like. "Right, I need one of those vol-au-vent things, I am famished."

When Indie has gone, Mum comes over to me.

"Looks good, doesn't it?" I say, indicating the decor.

Mum agrees. "They've done a really nice job of it."

"And Dad," I say. "He looks good too."

"Your father's doing really well," says Mum, smiling.

CLINK, CLINK, CLINK!

"Um, excuse me, ladies and gentlemen!"

Dad stands at the head of the room, smiling. He's holding a copy of his book. I've got mine already, all signed and personalized. It looks really good. The front cover has Carlos sprinting forward with a letter in his hand, pursued by hordes of microchip-brained zombies.

"Thank you," Dad says, when quiet descends. "Thank you all so much for coming. I'm truly overwhelmed that so many of you are here."

"I bet Peregrine is as well," says Lloyd. "We're probably breaking maximum occupancy regulations."

The posties in attendance laugh, while Peregrine grins good-naturedly and shifts from foot to foot.

"I'm going to read a little bit of the book to you in a moment, but before I do, I just want to talk about how important this whole thing has been for me."

I see Dad seeking out our faces in the crowd. Even from here, I can see his eyes twinkling under the fairy lights.

"A few years ago, I was miserable," he says. "And it was because I felt like a failure. I always dreamt of being a writer, and instead I was just a postman."

"No offence taken!" says Lloyd, earning another eruption of laughter.

"But this whole thing has made me realize I was wrong," says Dad. "There's nothing wrong with being just a postman. When you're a postman, you're a part of community life. You bring good news and bad. You're a listening ear to people who are lonely. You're a moving target for restless dogs." More laughter. "Over the years I became jaded and forgot that, but I never will again. And you can talk profits and efficiency and shareholders, but nothing will ever stop us providing that service to the community."

A round of applause ripples through the room.

"And there's another thing I was wrong about," says Dad. "I was looking outside for happiness, when it was with me all along: my family. They are what is truly important. Everything else is a distant second." He holds up the book. "I'm going to read a bit to you now. It's at the end. Now, I know I shouldn't read the last chapter, but pretty much all of you have read advance copies by now, seen yourself in it and agreed not to sue, so I suppose it doesn't matter." He stops and takes a deep breath. "Here we go."

The Aftermath

Carlos returned to the Badlands on his Harley, scarred and exhausted. He had failed to take down President McGuffin and his army of zombie drones and now it was time to return to his family. He hoped that by some miracle, they might have avoided being chipped.

He went to his old family house, but no one was home. Where were they? He couldn't call any of them because the President has jammed the communication networks in the entire area.

Carlos fell to his knees. Had he lost his family? How could he go on? He closed his eyes as the tears came. He thought he could hear a voice on the wind. It sounded like Indie. How cruel it was that his mind was playing tricks on him like that.

"Dad! Is that you?"

Carlos opened his eyes, and there, running towards him from the car, was his daughter. He jumped to his feet and ran to her, scooping her up in his arms just like he did when she was a little girl. She cried as they embraced.

"Oh, my baby girl. You haven't got the chip!"

"No!" she said. "Well, I did, but … oh, Dad, you need to get down to your depot. It's amazing."

"My depot?" said Carlos. "I don't understand."

Indie shook her head. "Neither do I, to be honest. Just get down there."

Kate stood some way back and greeted Carlos with a wave. "It's true," she said. "Alex has … well, you'll see."

Carlos was so relieved to see her, he wanted to hug her too but he decided not to. It didn't seem right.

Carlos went straight to the depot and opened the door. He expected to see piles of letters and parcels, but to his shock, there were none. What had Alex done?

A shadow flitted from behind some shelving at the back of the room, putting Carlos on high alert. But this was no zombie.

"Dad?" said Alex.

Carlos was so happy to see his boy, he scooped him up in his arms. Well, he tried to. He was too big for that now.

"What are you doing here?"

Alex looked a little uneasy. "Well, actually, Dad, while you were away, I've been helping out a little bit."

Carlos chuckled a little. "Really? How?"

Alex shrugged. "Oh, just delivering letters and parcels."

Carlos couldn't believe what he was hearing.

"You've been out in the desert? Delivering things?"

Alex nodded.

"In the heat? With the scorpions? And the snakes?"

Alex nodded again. To begin with, Carlos was angry. He could have been seriously hurt, or worse, but soon the anger gave way to pride, as bright and shiny as a new penny.

"What?" said Alex, wondering why his dad was staring at him like that.

"I don't know," said Carlos. "I suppose I was stuck thinking of you as a little boy, when actually you're a young man now."

Alex blushed. He hadn't thought of it like that. He did it to help, to keep the Badlands going in his father's absence.

"I've got to ask, though," said Carlos. "How did you get around?"

Alex smiled. "Come on, I'll show you," he said.

Carlos followed Alex through the depot to the back yard. There, propped up by the wall, was an old moped, with a dented helmet hanging off it.

"Found it back here," said Alex.

Carlos laughed. "You're amazing, do you know that?"

Alex blushed harder but didn't speak.

"There's one thing I don't get, though," said Carlos. "Why were letter deliveries needed when everyone in the Badlands was fitted with chips?"

Alex laughed bashfully. "Oh yeah. I figured out a way around that."

Carlos's eyes widened. "What do you mean?"

"Well, I was being attacked by Christmas Mickey one day, and just as he was about to grab me, I moved out of the way and his hand hit an electric fence. As soon as it happened, he smiled and started saying "Merry Christmas" again. And I tried it again with other people. Same result every time. The electric must overload the chip and stop it working."

Carlos screamed with laughter and once again pulled his son in for a hug. "Brilliant!" he cried. "This changes everything!"

A minute later, the two of them were speeding off across the Badlands, Carlos on his Harley and Alex on his moped. Carlos knew Lloyd needed to hear about this discovery, then another fight back could begin.

Carlos watched his boy weave in and out of potholes and discarded tyres and he smiled through his tears. He always thought that parenting was a one-way street, and that it would always be him helping his kids, sending them down the right path, but now he saw that wasn't the case. He had given up in despair, convinced the world was about to end. But in his son, he could see hope. He could see a way forward.

There, right in front of him was the purpose to his life he had been searching for the whole time. The best job in the world wasn't a millionaire CEO, or any kind of swaggering bigshot. It was being a dad, and nothing could ever take that away from him.

While the audience applauds, Willow reaches over and squeezes my hand, giving me a warm, reassuring smile. I smile back a little, but I'm too choked and I'm probably making a silly face she'll definitely make fun of later.

I've come to realize over the past year that my view of the Natural Order of Things was all wrong. I thought everything had to go a certain way, and then I thought they never could, so there was no such thing as a Natural Order of Things. But there *is* a Natural Order of Things: change.

Like a tiny twig on the shoulders of a mighty stream.

And that isn't so bad. Maybe.

As the applause turns into whoops and cheers, I turn and see Dad smile at Mum. It's a thin smile, but it's warm and full of love. I look up and see Mum returning it. I remember what she said last year about making the best of what you have, about starting with the foundations and building from there, and I can't help but wonder if our foundations are a little stronger than I thought.

I don't know what we'll build on them.

But I'm excited to find out.

was a much more personal experience than usual, particularly the passages about a tired postman struggling to write a book, but Linas got me through it. I should also shout out everyone at Scholastic. It's just my name on the cover, but there's a much bigger team behind the scenes that really make things happen.

Thanks as ever to my agent, Penny Holroyde for being my rock in the stormy seas of the book biz.

I couldn't write one of these things without mentioning my wonderful family. Hester and Dougie, you are my reason for getting up in the morning. Literally, in Dougie's case. The boy is always awake at the crack of dawn.

Elodie, as I write this, you're a bump, but by the time this book is out, you will be an actual baby. Let's hope you don't look too much like your old man, sweetheart.

Finally, I would be remiss not to acknowledge all my postie colleagues, past and present. You do an important job, and I hope this book has done that justice. Don't let them grind you down.

Acknowledgements

When it was first suggested to me to write a book about a kid who becomes a postman, I had literally no idea how to make it entertaining. After all, it's ultimately stuffing paper through doors. But then I thought about all the eccentric characters I'd encountered over the years, many of whom are colleagues, and I realized I had a way in.

That was only the beginning though, because doing that led me to think deeply about the role of the postie in the community, going back hundreds of years, and I realized that this would be a story about friendship, family and connection.

Thanks to Linas Alsenas for his invaluable editorial assistance, not to mention suggesting the idea in the first place! Working on this story